Her Secret Sheik

The Book Club

Elizabeth Lennox

Copyright 2022
ISBN13: 9798426656505
All rights reserved

This is a work of fiction. Names, characters, businesses, places, events, and incidents are either the product of the author's imagination or used in a fictitious manner. Any resemblance to actual persons, living or dead, or actual events is purely coincidental. Any duplication of this material, either electronic or any other format, either currently in use or a future invention, is strictly prohibited, unless you have the direct consent of the author.

Table of Contents

Chapter 1	1
Chapter 2	17
Chapter 3	24
Chapter 4	34
Chapter 5	38
Chapter 6	44
Chapter 7	49
Chapter 8	56
Chapter 9	65

Chapter 10	76
Chapter 11	84
Chapter 12	90
Chapter 13	94
Chapter 14	98
Epilogue	113
Excerpt from "The Sheik's Redemption"	116

Chapter 1

The stupid frills were in the way! Twelve year old Amilee hated the dress her mother had chosen. She hated walking down the long ceremonial room, and she hated her parents for betrothing her to a man she despised!

Deep down, Amilee knew she didn't *really* hate any of...okay, she truly hated the ridiculous dress. But her anger was really just a cover for nervousness. But seriously, no one wanted to walk down a stupid red carpet towards one's "betrothed". Amilee didn't really understand what a "betrothed" was. Did her parents truly expect her to marry someone she'd never even met?

And why would anyone want to marry her, or "betroth" her, when she was wearing a stupid, pink dress with more layers of ruffles and frills than a china doll...and it made her look stupid! She was finally twelve years old, and yet, her mother had forced her to wear this idiotic dress and...! Amilee had argued with her mother, begging her to select a dress that didn't make her look like a cupcake! And pink! Good grief, only little girls wore pink!

Amilee tugged at the hem of her dress, wishing the hem ended at her knees or down at her toes. Wearing a dress that ended right above her anklebones made her feel so awkward. In her opinion, the length of the dress looked like she'd grown half a foot and no one had bothered to let out the hem! She felt stupid. She looked stupid. And Amilee really didn't get what all the fuss was about.

A tall, dark haired jerk walked down the steps from the dais. Amilee eyed him curiously, wondering why he looked so stiff and...boring. And tall. The guy was definitely tall!

She looked up into his dark, dark eyes and...and nothing, because the guy ignored her, facing forward. Thankfully, he didn't try to touch her.

Ick! Amilee turned and gazed up at Sheik What's-his-name, trying to remember everything she was supposed to do during the ceremony. Fortunately, her main job was to stand still while the man off to the right spouted some nonsense about "sacred promises" and "forever bound". She didn't understand and didn't really care.

Unfortunately, her eyes kept flitting to the man standing beside her looking so formal and scary. She supposed he was handsome enough, if one liked the dark and dangerous type. The dark hair and dark eyes were…fine. Unfortunately, the irises of his eyes were so dark that Amilee couldn't differentiate his irises from the rest of his eyes. Also, she had dark hair and dark eyes. So…whatever. The guy standing next to her was fine, she conceded. He wasn't like the singer in her new favorite group. The lead singer in "Flaming Ferns", Tim Coltar, had blue eyes and soft, full lips.

"Ms. Amilee Lahgami," the dour faced man standing on the dais bellowed so that the whole room could hear, "Do you willingly accept this betrothal, under no duress?"

Amilee quaked in her pink satin shoes. She tilted her head back to look up at the man. He was so tall. Or maybe she was just incredibly short. He looked down his long, thin nose at her and, when Amilee hesitated, he lifted a dark, sardonic eyebrow. She pulled her eyes away and searched for her mother. Seeing her nod, Amilee sighed inwardly, remembering the rehearsals she'd gone through over the past few days. Turning back to the loud doofus in front of her, she nodded. "Yes," she stated clearly, remembering her father's instructions that she had to speak her agreement loudly so that everyone in the room behind her could hear. Witnesses. She didn't understand any of this so…whatever, she mentally rolled her eyes. Agreeing seemed like the easiest way to finish this so she could find the cake that had been promised to her. She'd even gotten to choose the flavor this time! Lemon! Lemon cake was her favorite!

Thankfully, when she uttered the "right" words, the man in front of her stopped glowering and lifted his eyes to look at the man beside her. "And do you, Prince Rian al Sayed, accept the terms of this betrothal?"

Beside her, the annoying man's voice boomed loud and clear. "I accept."

In front of her, the loud guy nodded, beaming his approval as he raised his hand. The large and ornate gold ring on the man's finger transfixed Amilee. She remembered someone explaining that the ring was important and only worn during significant ceremonies. Amilee thought the heavy, gold ring was ugly, but kept her opinion to herself. The man gestured for both her and the guy beside her to step forward. Her father and Sheik Safir al Sayed, Rian's father, stepped forward as well.

"Sign here, dear." Someone put a pen in her hand, but Amilee was looking at the Sheik. He didn't look happy. Or maybe he just didn't feel good. There was a grey tinge to his skin that reminded her of someone she'd seen in the hospital last year.

"Right here, Amilee," her father urged, pointing to a line on the wrinkled-looking document. The pen was heavy and decorative. She'd practiced signing her name with it yesterday. She stared at the document. Unfortunately, she was so nervous with so many people watching her and the line…she couldn't actually *see* the line. Amilee's mother cleared her throat. Amilee knew that her mother wanted her to sign the document. They'd practiced over and over! But not with an audience.

With a heavy sigh, Amilee peeked up through her lashes at the man beside her. He looked confused and concerned with her hesitation. Amilee sighed and reached into her dress pocket, pulling her glasses out. Sliding them onto her nose, she looked down at the document and, with relief, was able to see the line where she was supposed to sign. "Sorry," she whispered, picking up the heavy, ceremonial pen as she carefully signed her name, unaware of her tongue peeking out of the corner of her mouth as she focused.

When she finished, Amilee was proud of the delicate scrawl and stepped back, waiting as her father signed right below her name. Apparently, he had to sign as well because she was too young, which didn't make sense to her at all. When this had been explained to her yesterday, she'd asked why she was being betrothed if she was too young, but everyone had simply chuckled as if she'd asked a silly question.

Then it was her "betrothed's" turn to sign the document. Crown Prince Rian leaned down and scribbled his signature, obviously not nearly as concerned with his penmanship as she'd been. Nor did he have trouble with the heavy pen, which really annoyed Amilee. Was she the only one in this room that struggled with this stuff?

He stepped back, handing the pen to his father. The handsome ruler of Abidnae signed his name as a witness. It also irritated Amilee that Rian's father only had to witness everyone's signature while her father had to sign his agreement under her signature. That didn't seem fair, but…whatever. Rian was twenty years old, so he was legally an adult. It still didn't make sense that she could be "betrothed" at such a young age to a man who was already in college. It sounded ridiculous, but her parents had explained what a "delightful privilege" this was for Amilee. She didn't feel "delighted"! Plus, standing here in front of all of these people who were staring at her, wearing a giant, frilly, pink dress…

she didn't feel as if this was any great "privilege" either. In her mind, this whole scene was just a big pain in the butt! Yes, she knew that she wasn't supposed to say "butt". However, she hadn't said it. She'd only thought it! And no one could control her thoughts, she reminded herself with increasing resentment.

As soon as all the signatures were done, the older man turned to the crowd and lifted his hands. "The betrothal is official. Let us celebrate!"

There was a round of polite applause, as if Amilee and Rian had done something stupendous, instead of simply signing their names on a piece of paper. But Amilee didn't care. She was hungry. She wanted that promised lemon cake! Amilee also knew there were cheese puffs on the menu and strawberry lemonade. She was eager to try both, but she'd also been told that she needed to stand here, waiting for the annoying applause to die down.

Thankfully, the ornate, double doors opened and a bevy of servants appeared wearing immaculate livery in the blue and gold of Abidnae, carrying heavy trays filled with sparkling champagne. The crowd who had patiently witnessed the ceremony, cheered more for the champagne than the stupid signing ceremony, percolating in Amilee's mind that whatever she'd just signed couldn't have been all that important. The servants hurriedly passed out champagne, barely needing to move since the crowd of gawkers surged towards the sparkling stuff like a tidal wave. Amilee didn't like champagne, and eagerly watched for a servant carrying a tray of the promised lemonade!

"You did an excellent job!" her father told her, placing a hand briefly on her back. Amilee smiled up at her father, feeling a rush of pride. Her father was a good man, tall and proud, and Amilee knew that he was an important member of Sheik Sayed's government. "Thanks Dad," she whispered.

Amilee searched the crowd, finding her mother smiling and laughing among a group of other women. Suppressing the familiar stab of pain, Amilee turned away. Her mother had never been the "motherly" type, as her father had said on several occasions. Amilee told herself that she should be relieved that her mother was safely occupied. If her mother bothered to speak with Amilee, she would probably list all the things she'd done wrong during the ceremony. Including pulling out her glasses!

The dark-eyed man, Rian,..her "betrothed"...looked down and offered her a patronizing smile. "I was impressed, Amilee."

Aimlee smiled crookedly, not sure what she'd done that was so great. All she'd done is answer a question and sign her name. Seemed like a stupid ceremony to her. But she knew she should be polite, so she replied with an appropriate, "Thank you," and added a small curtsy. Her mother had forced her to practice her curtsies over and over. Thankfully, Amilee didn't tip over and embarrass herself this time, although she'd looked ridiculous during her practice sessions over the past few days. But even if she had fallen over, no one would have noticed. The guests were moving towards the buffet lines. It also seemed as if everyone had a glass of bubbly champagne in hand, and yet, she still couldn't see a waiter with the lemonade! This was so unfair!

Amilee's impatience must have come through on her features because her mother broke away from her friends. "I know you're hungry, dear," her mother whispered, patting Amilee's shoulder. "As the guests of honor, you'll have to wait until the witnesses are served."

Amilee sighed. She didn't like this "betrothal" business. Seemed like a lot of fuss about nothing to her.

Rian smothered his amusement at his "betrothed's" obvious irritation. She was a tiny little thing. Only twelve years old. Several months ago, when his father had presented the betrothal contract for Rian's review, he'd found himself hesitating, arguing that a twelve year old child shouldn't be bound to a stranger for the rest of her life. Rian and his father had discussed the issue at length and his concerns had been appeased, and yet, today, those misgivings had resurfaced. Stating that the girl's family had explained everything and that this was just the normal way of arranging a marriage had seemed fine previously, but seeing Amilee now, seeing her obvious confusion, he wasn't sure anymore. It didn't seem…right.

"So, you're betrothed," a sarcastic, feminine voice called out.

Rian turned to find his college friends approaching, champagne glasses in hand, although most of those glasses were already empty.

Rian turned, offering his arm to the small girl beside him, trying to include her while at the same time, giving his friends a quelling look. He'd invited his friends here for the weekend, forgetting that they weren't from his country and thus didn't understand the ancient traditions his country embraced. As the future leader of his country, Rian understood those traditions and grasped the importance of the rituals for his people, even if he didn't fully agree with them. His friends…not so much.

"Amilee, these are my school friends," he explained, putting a protective hand on her shoulder. "This is Roger, Andrea, Razeen, and Phillip." He turned to his friends, "Everyone, this is my betrothed, Amilee."

Roger was the first to step forward, extending his hand with a gallant bow. "Amilee, it is a pleasure to meet you. You're far braver than I, my dear." Roger gave Amilee a playful wink, brushed a kiss to her knuckles, then released her hand as he stepped back, rejoining the group.

Roger was a follower, Rian thought, restraining himself from taking Amilee's hand in his and wiping Roger's kiss away. He definitely was not a leader, and perhaps a bit of a friend-leech. But he'd been kind to Amilee and that counted for something.

Andrea snickered, but quickly masked her amusement when Rian glared at her. When she then stepped closer, her features were the epitome of kindness and respect as Andrea extended her hand to Amilee as well. "Your dress is lovely," Andrea said as she shook Amilee's hand.

Rian could feel Amilee move closer to him and he looked down, caught Amilee taking in Andrea's sophisticated sheath dress that fit her athletic frame like a glove and wished that he could do something, say something, to make Amilee feel better about her pink dress. It was a bit…well, it wasn't particularly flattering for her petite frame.

If Rian needed another hint that his newly betrothed felt self-conscious, Amilee tugged at one of the ruffles on her dress. Rian just knew she hated the dress. He suspected that Andrea knew it too, and was just being her normal slightly bitchy self by bringing it up.

But that was Andrea. He'd never been entirely comfortable with Andrea's snarky comments, but she was a lot of fun most of the time. If she had an occasionally irritating habit of belittling others, well, she kept it hidden most of the time.

Phillip stepped up next and bowed to Amilee. "Amilee, you are a lovely young lady." He paused to wink at her. "You will make a beautiful princess some day."

Amilee's eyes narrowed and Rian fought down a chuckle. Obviously, Amilee didn't like the idea of being a princess! How odd!

Razeen stepped forward and he could see the malicious intent glinting in her eyes. "Don't!" he snapped, stepping closer to Amilee as if he could somehow protect her from Razeen's inevitably harsh words. Razeen was superficially beautiful, but she could be malicious when she felt snubbed.

Razeen's eyes met his, blinking innocently. "I was only going to congratulate her on her betrothal!" she replied in a breathy voice. It was the odd smile afterward that Rian didn't like.

Razeen bent down, hands braced on her knees, as if she were talking to a toddler. "When you grow up, you're going to be a very important person because of your connection to Rian." She winked and straightened up, then shot a sultry look at Rian. He understood that look and shuddered. Yes, he and Razeen had been more than friends at one time. But no longer. He'd broken things off with her several months ago, although Razeen hadn't fully agreed that the intimate aspect of their friendship was over.

"Come on, everyone," Razeen called out, dangling her empty champagne glass in the air with delicate fingers that showed off her bright red manicure. "Let's go find more booze!"

The others laughed, following Razeen away. Rian gritted his teeth, irritated by their behavior. On the surface, each had greeted Amilee politely. But he'd heard the undercurrents of amusement.

With a sigh, he turned back to his young betrothed. "I'm sorry about that, Amilee," he said when they were "alone". "They're usually more… polite than that."

Amilee sighed, smoothing a hand self-consciously down over the multiple layers of ruffles. Her tiny chin lifted slightly, as if she were trying to gird herself against the memory of his friends' comments.

But Amilee merely shrugged, dismissing the subtle insults. "It's okay. They're just jealous that I'm your betrothed. Especially Razeen." She lifted her soft, brown gaze up to meet his and he was struck by the intelligence in that gaze. "She wants to be your girlfriend."

Stunned, Rian had to remind himself that she was only twelve and not the twenty-something that her insightful comment indicated. Rian's gaze moved from Razeen's bony, retreating shoulders down to Amilee, surprised by her understanding of the situation. When he looked up again, Razeen was glancing over her shoulder in a "come hither" pose.

"You are very perceptive," he said. When he glanced down at her again, Amilee was looking around, craning her neck as if searching for something.

Amilee sighed with what he suspected was resignation. "There's only champagne to drink."

He glanced down at her again. "Would you like some?" He wouldn't allow it, of course, but he was startled to find himself fascinated by this girl-child who would eventually become his wife. They'd met briefly before this signing ceremony, but he hadn't really spoken to her. There hadn't been time to have actual conversations. Besides, how could he truly converse with a girl eight years his junior? Her world was still evolving and changing so rapidly, her opinion about a subject today might be completely different tomorrow. Which had been one of his arguments against this betrothal. But Rian's father had waved the argument away, explaining that his betrothal would provide reassurance to the people in their country, guaranteeing them succession of their family line.

"Champagne?" she whispered in horror. Amilee squinched up her nose. "No way!" she gasped. "That stuff is gross!"

He laughed, delighted with this girl-woman. "Well, then what would you like?"

Amilee looked around, obviously not happy with the view. He saw the moment that she decided not to tell him. "I'm fine," she stated, her shoulders drooping ever so slightly. But he grasped that she wasn't "fine". She was irritated or disappointed about something and trying to hide it.

Normally, Rian would have dropped it. But there was something about Amilee, a strength and tenacity hidden beneath all those hideous ruffles. He wanted...to protect her? Yes, but that wasn't exactly it at the moment. He wanted...to make her happy. Yes, that was exactly it! He wanted to bring a smile to her face. He wanted to bring back that shimmering smile that he'd had a brief glimpse of a moment ago.

Rian touched her shoulder. "Why don't we sneak out to the kitchen and grab our own feast?" he suggested.

Amilee's eyes widened in surprised delight. Quickly, she looked around as if trying to determine if anyone else milling about would catch them doing something so illegal. "Can we really do that?" she asked, quivering slightly with hope. "My parents told me that I had to stay here and speak with anyone who wanted to talk with me." Her fingers tightened into little fists, rumpling her dress. "They had me rehearse replies to different questions."

He laughed, nodding his head. "Yeah, my governess did that for me when I was about your age. It's good practice. But in this case," he looked around, suddenly repulsed by the way everyone was laughing and guzzling the excellent champagne, "no one seems to want to talk with us. So why don't we get out of here? I think we've been the center of attention long enough, don't you?"

Amilee grinned eagerly at the suggestion and Rian was startled by the dramatic change in her appearance. Gone was the serious girl-child who had been lectured and schooled for her first major public appearance, and in her place came the gamin, adorable child with cute dimples and sparkling, chocolate eyes, more than ready for mischief!

"I'd love to!" she laughed.

He glanced around, nodded to his father who understood the silent message, then gestured to Amilee, leading her towards the doors that would take them to the kitchens.

Pushing through a set of double doors, the noise increased exponentially under the bright, white lights where the palace kitchen staff rushed about. Orders were bellowed, pots and pans clanged, and, in the distance, something clattered to the floor. There were about thirty people bustling about. Chefs, waiters, line cooks, and sous chefs all called out orders to one another. It was organized chaos and a completely different environment from the civilly elegant affair they'd just left.

"Cheese puffs!" Amilee whispered, unconsciously licking her lips and inching closer to Rian. A steaming tray of golden cheese puffs had just been pulled out of an oven and placed on a rack to cool. The treat was right in front of them and Amilee was almost bouncing with excitement.

"Cheese puffs it is," he announced, wanting to give the poor kid a treat. He grabbed a plate, and proceeded to fill one side of it with the still-warm cheese puffs. "What else?" he asked, looking down at her and ignoring the kitchen staff who were surprised to find a royal prince in their midst.

Rian noticed that Amilee kept her hands tucked behind her back, as if she'd been ordered not to touch anything.

"What about some of these?" he asked, taking a pair of tongs and adding several small cakes and confectionaries on the plate. One of the chefs noticed them and started to open his mouth. But Rian gave the man a look that dared him to object. Thankfully, another of the other kitchen staff rushed over and whispered in the man's ear, obviously explaining who Rian was.

Amilee pointed at the various treats and Rian piled the plate high with appetizers. When they were done, he stopped a waiter and asked for glasses of lemonade to be brought to them.

"You don't have to drink lemonade," she told him, her chocolate eyes serious and almost sad again. "You can have the champagne, if you'd like. I promise I don't mind." She bit her lip and toyed with the ruffles on her dress. "I know lemonade is a kid's drink."

Rian could see the insecurity in her eyes and his heart went out to the girl. Smiling gently, he didn't wait for the waiter to bring them the treat. Instead, he poured two glasses of lemonade from a large, ice-filled pitcher. "I like lemonade," he lied. "It's refreshing. You carry the drinks and I have the appetizers."

He led her through a different door this time. This one led out to the palace courtyard. Since it was dark now, the lights of the palace were lit up and they could easily see what was going on. "Let's sit down over there," he said, indicating a bench under a tree. He put the plate between them, then chose a cheese puff, popping it in his mouth and nodding his approval. "Good choice!"

She smiled, relaxing as she picked up a puff. "Oh, they're so good!" she sighed, slouching for the first time.

"So…you're in college?" she asked. When he nodded, she sipped her lemonade. "What are you studying?"

He looked at her curiously. "You don't know?"

She shrugged self-consciously. "I was given a big binder filled with information about you." She fluttered a hand over those damn ruffles again. "I was supposed to memorize it. But I didn't want to know the facts," she explained, tilting her head slightly. "I doubt the facts in that binder are the real you. I don't like it when someone summarizes my personality, as if I'm one thing or another. It never sounds like *me*. I think that people are more complex than a summary of facts." She picked up another cheese puff and looked up at him. "So," she tilted her head, "what are you studying?"

"Economics," he told her.

She nodded. "And do you enjoy it?"

Rian was startled by her question. Looking at her curiously, he replied, "No one has ever asked me that before."

Those pretty, dark eyebrows shot up and, for the first time, he noticed how exotic her eyes were. "Well, do you?" she prompted.

He laughed, shaking his head at her curiosity. "I guess so." He shrugged and took a long sip of the lemonade. It was pretty good, actually! "I've never really thought about it. I need to understand economics in order to rule my country better, so I take the classes."

She nodded and Rian suspected that there was a wealth of understanding in that gesture. "I want to study women's social history," she announced. "A lot of people think that one can trace the history of the world and understand each region's culture by studying wars."

He'd heard that argument before and nodded. "That is the general consensus, I believe."

She shrugged and chose another tiny cake. "I don't agree." She took a delicate bite, lowering the remainder to the napkin in her lap. She looked like a fairy, he thought suddenly.

Shaking off such fanciful thoughts, he returned to their conversation. "Why is that?"

She sighed. "Because wars were traditionally fought by men. And if we only study the wars, then we miss out on half of the world's history." She saw him consider this and pressed on. "I think we should study social history, especially *women's* social history. I think we can learn more about life and why we are where we are if we study what led to a war. What events and cultural issues pushed two countries, tribes, or nations to the point where violence was necessary? We should study what happens during peace times within a community and region, not just before, during, and immediately after a war. What were people thinking? What were their hopes and dreams? Are they even allowed hopes and dreams or are those crushed under a dictator? We should study the people, not just the rulers. It's the commoners who push for change and encourage culture to evolve over time. Understanding the commoners also helps us understand the leaders. Why do so many people follow a leader into battle? What's the mental momentum that brings people to that point?"

She stopped when she saw him smiling at her and sighed, deflating once again as she stared down at the uneaten portion of her tiny cake. "I know. Boring subject."

He laughed softly and pushed the plate towards her, silently offering her the last few cheese puffs. "Not at all. In fact, I've never thought about it that way. You might have a point."

She lifted her eyes anxiously. But at the sincerity in his expression, Amilee's lovely features morphed into a beautiful smile, her relief evident. A moment later, Amilee looked out into the darkness. "I love social history. I think it's so much more interesting than studying about how humanity has learned to kill people more efficiently." She lifted her eyes to him again. "So, why do you like economics?" She popped another cheese puff into her mouth.

"I like numbers. And although economics is a lot of math, one also needs to understand social norms and reactions behind the numbers. I enjoy the more humanitarian aspect of that math curriculum."

She wiped her fingers on the napkin. "That's interesting. And are you good at it?"

He laughed, delighted with her openness. "Most people just assume that I'm excellent at everything I do," he admonished with a teasing voice.

She squinched here nose again. "I know," she replied with a giggle. There was a sparkle of mischief in her eyes as she continued. "That was bad of me, wasn't it? I'm supposed to be more reverent to your every word, to bow and scrape, and…" she sighed, batting at the irritating ruffles now. "And I'm supposed to hang on your every word." She looked up at him, her eyes turning serious. "You don't mind if I don't do that, do you? I'm not good at it. And I'd probably lose a great deal of respect for you if you demanded it of me." She angled her head slightly. "And isn't it better to be respected than revered?"

The teasing comment he was going to give died on his lips. Rian was stunned. And impressed! Slowly, as if he couldn't understand how a child of twelve could have such a brilliant grasp of life, he nodded his head. "Yes, I'd have to agree with you there. And no, I don't want you to bow and scrape to me." It was true, he thought. He absolutely hated the stupid ways that people bowed to him. "I don't want a submissive wife."

She grinned, those charming dimples reappearing. "You don't want a wife at all! And I don't want a husband." Her eyes brightened, looking as if she'd just solved one of the great mysteries of the universe. "So, we're perfectly matched!" and she picked up the last of the small cakes, nibbling delicately.

He chuckled. "You're right there. Marriage is…difficult, even when two people are madly in love." He looked away, staring into the darkness. "But it's the way of our people. And everyone is thrilled that you've agreed to marry me. Eventually."

She laughed, rolling her eyes. "Puleese! The entire country is jealous that I'm your betrothed. Most of the women, especially your friends, would stab me in the back and step over my body in order to reach you, Your Highness."

She was so cute, he thought with a chuckle. "I hope it never comes to that. But you'll be protected, Amilee."

She shrugged, obviously unconcerned.

"Your Highness," a man in a dark suit called out.

Rian turned, his eyes sharpening on the man. "It's happening?"

The man nodded.

Rian looked back at Amilee. "My apologies, Amilee," he said to her, taking her hand in his as he stood up. "I have to leave now. I look forward to our next meeting." And he bowed over her hand, kissing her fingers in a very old-world style gesture before walking away with the stranger.

As she watched him stride away, disappearing along the dark pathway, Amilee's smile faded and she wondered what she should do next. Looking around, she contemplated the silence and the darkness, the fluttering stars overhead and the confusing events of the day. Instead of heading back into the ballroom where everyone would stare at her and whisper behind their hands, probably making rude comments about her stupid dress, Amilee remained on the bench, watching the people move about the ceremonial room with drinks and food, laughing and enjoying themselves. Oblivious that one of the guests of honor was outside, watching everything through the glass doors. A light turned on to her right and she noticed Rian walking into a room. There were several men already there and they looked serious. They didn't completely close the doors and she watched as they discussed something very seriously.

Amilee pulled her eyes away from the room, feeling as if she might be invading Rian's privacy by watching. Besides, the moon was beautiful tonight. It illuminated the flowers blooming in the courtyard and shimmered off some of the hardier leaves. Sitting here on this bench, with the branches of the tree overhead, she felt as if she were in a secret world. A private world. The floral scents and the soft chirping of cicadas gave her a sense of...peace.

"You've found my favorite hiding place."

Amilee startled, watching an elderly woman sit down on the other end of the bench. She had silver hair pulled up into a bun on top of her head and she wore a sparkling outfit that looked more like a caftan than a dress. It was elegant "bohemian", which suited the woman's hip jewelry perfectly. Again, Amilee glanced down at her own pink, ruffled atrocity and sighed, wondering when she'd be allowed to choose her own clothes and figure out her own "style".

"You're Amilee, aren't you?" the elderly woman asked, sighing as she carefully settled herself onto the stone bench. Her weathered hands clasped an ornate cane, the rings on her fingers shimmering in the dim light as she folded them over the top. The woman sighed as she relaxed against the bench, smiling at...something that obviously made her happy.

Still staring up at the stars, she patted Amilee's hand. "In a few years, you will be my granddaughter-in-law, so you may call me Inis," she commanded regally.

Amilee smiled politely at the woman, not sure if she was crazy or just kind. Either was possible, she knew. "Thank you, Inis."

The woman's eyes moved over Amilee, a gentle look in her eyes. "You hate that dress, don't you?" It was said in a conspiratorial whisper and, for a moment, Amilee wasn't sure she'd heard Inis correctly.

Amilee nodded with a short laugh. "Yes. It's ridiculous. My mother told me that the dress was appropriate for today's ceremony, but I just feel silly."

Inis laughed softly. "It's quite a study in ruffles." Her gaze moved towards the ballroom. "I suspect that the original architect of this courtyard wanted to impress palace guests with the view of the plants and trees, hence the walls of windows and doors along the three sides of the courtyard. But no one inside realizes how much can be seen from out here at night. It's a beautiful place to come and watch the activities that are happening inside." She chuckled. "The views are the reason that this bench is my favorite place to sit at night."

Amilee smiled her agreement, but remained quiet, watching the guests inside while she sat outside under the stars. Everyone in the ballroom was laughing and appeared to be having a wonderful time. Amilee felt like an outsider, almost as if she were looking at a microscope of her life.

"You're going to be a beautiful woman, Amilee," Inis proclaimed softly, interrupting Amilee's melancholy thoughts. She sighed heavily, her fingers twisting on the top of the cane's handle. "You're just a child, and you shouldn't have become betrothed at such a young age. You have so much life to live before you commit yourself to one man and one goal." She paused, her eyes returning to the stars. "But I have a feeling about you," she said with a smile and a confident nod. "I think there is going to be a wonderful romance in your life."

Again, Amilee smiled politely, wondering what could be so wonderful about her future life. She was betrothed to a man who…who had understood how lonely her world was, stolen treats with her, and talked to her, laughed with her. And then disappeared to do something more important.

Her eyes darted towards the door and she wondered if anyone would ever consider her to be "more important". The room through which Rian had disappeared was closed now, so she couldn't see him. Then her eyes shifted towards the glass windows looking into the elegant ballroom where perhaps two hundred people were celebrating her betrothal. No one other than this kind, elderly woman knew that she was out here. Everyone was completely unaware of her absence. In other words, she wasn't important to their celebration either.

She thought about Inis' proclamation, wondering if the "romance" would be with her husband to be. Her eyes drifted to the windows in front of the closed door. No, one had to be important to someone before anything fabulous could happen.

Rian tried to listen to the other three men. They were discussing an infrastructure issue with the northern territories and funding issues with a contractor. But in reality, Rian's mind kept returning to the twelve year old girl-child sitting alone outside on a cold, marble bench. He wanted to tell these men to figure out the issue on their own. Or maybe he could tell them to discuss it tomorrow morning. Every instinct warned him that Amilee needed him.

"Son, this is your domain," his father said, interrupting his thoughts. "You mentioned that the region needs more bridges, and that would take some of the pressure off the…" Rian's father continued to speak, but Rian wanted to tell him that he had more important things to do. Amilee needed him!

Which was ridiculous! Amilee was a beautiful, confident twelve year old. She was more poised than any twelve year old should be! Hell, she should be out doing…what the hell did twelve year old girls do? He had no clue, but he was positive that normal twelve year olds shouldn't have to handle a formal betrothal to a man she barely knew. And yet,

Amilee had gone through the betrothal ceremony as if she'd been born to the role.

So, what would Amilee be doing if she weren't here? Or out sitting in the darkness, all alone, staring up at the stars? Even when he'd been twelve years old, he hadn't understood what girls his age were up to. He still didn't know, even now. In all honesty, he didn't have time to wonder what women normally did.

So what was it about Amilee that worried him so much? She'd obviously been trained for today's betrothal ceremony and, besides that stupid pink dress, she'd done a stellar job. Everyone commented about what a beautiful little girl she was, how poised and "ready to take on the challenges she'd face in the future". And yet, Rian had sensed a vulnerability within her. There was strength too. And tenacity! He'd felt the tremble when he'd touched her shoulder during the ceremony. He'd seen the fear and confusion in her eyes. And yet, when she'd needed her glasses, she'd ignored the horrified gasp from her mother and donned them anyway.

Rian glanced at the doorway, wondering if anyone would know if he walked out and went back to Amilee. Just to check on her. Just to see her and get her to smile one more time.

"Rian!" his father called out.

Rian turned back to the group. They were staring at him, obviously waiting for him to issue commands that would resolve the infrastructure problem. With a sigh, he moved towards his father's massive desk where a map of the northern territories was spread out. Bracing his hands on the desk, he mentally shook himself, forcing himself to focus on the present problem and not on the lonely, little girl sitting out on the bench.

"We could…" and he explained a plan, his agile mind shifting priorities.

An hour later, all four men nodded in agreement, the crisis averted. "That sounds like an excellent plan," his father stated, slapping Rian's shoulder with approval. "Thank you!"

The other men also nodded in agreement, smiling with relief that the situation wouldn't spiral into a crisis.

"I need to go," Rian announced, ignoring the startled glances as his father began pouring whiskey. The other men were all sitting in the worn, leather chairs, eager to relax and enjoy a spot of whiskey and bask in their own importance and the masculine décor, far away from superfluous pillows and dainty champagne flutes.

Stepping out of the office, he hurried down the hallway towards the door that would lead to the courtyard. But as soon as he stepped out into the chilly night air, Rian knew that Amilee was gone. The girl who would eventually become his wife was no longer sitting on the bench and...oddly, Rian felt a stab of disappointment.

Ridiculous, he told himself as he walked over to the bench. It wasn't as if...as if what? Amilee was going to be a great beauty. From their kitchen pilfering and conversation, he also knew that she was intelligent and lively. She didn't need him, a boring, tedious guy she barely knew, to worry about her. She could take care of herself, he thought and leaned back, gazing up at the stars. He'd lived all of his life knowing that his future was mapped out for him. Centuries of traditions allowed Rian to anticipate where he would attend boarding school and college, what he would study, what he would eventually do as an adult. Even his hobbies had been anticipated. He learned languages and horseback riding, fencing and self-defense. He knew how to dance a waltz, charm diplomats, and understand world politics.

Did Amilee *truly* understand what she had signed today? That her life would be a predictable series of events and activities?

Even as he thought about how much her life would change once they were married, Rian tried to figure out ways to protect Amilee, to provide as much freedom as possible. Even if that was a pointless exercise in frustration.

Chapter 2

Two Years Later…

"Happy birthday, Amilee," Rian announced with a formal bow as he handed her a small, beautifully wrapped package. "Do you feel different now that you're officially fourteen?"

Startled, Amilee looked up from the cold, hard bench. She'd come out here to be alone, to escape the superficial smiles of the guests, all of whom had superficially come to celebrate her birthday. There was a table full of beautifully wrapped presents for her and there had been a lavish dinner, with grand toasts for her health and future, to which Amilee had drunk the lemonade while everyone around her toasted with cheers and champagne. Amilee had been seated in between her mother and father, neither of whom had spoken a word to her during dinner, preferring to converse with the others seated at their table instead.

"How did you know I'd be out here?" she asked, scooting over to make room for him on their bench. He sat down and she felt a warmth invade her. This felt special. He was a nice man and she was finally fourteen! Granted, he hadn't contacted her much over the past two years, even though she'd sent him letters and gifts for his birthday. Okay, perhaps she'd been ordered to write him letters. And Amilee acknowledged that the letters had been a bit…stiffly worded. But still, her mother demanded that she write him a letter every month, updating him on her studies.

In return, Amilee received a politely worded missive from Rian every few months.

This, she thought as he smiled down at her…this made her feel better about all of those stupid letters!

He smiled at her as he handed her a small box with a pink bow on top.

"I saw you sneaking out of the party and suspected you'd be out here." He nodded at the box. "Go ahead and open it."

She looked down, toying with the pretty bow. "I like to savor the anticipation of a present." She tilted her head slightly. "Holding it for a few moments, wondering what is underneath the pretty paper and bow, adds to the excitement, don't you think?"

His soft chuckle was deep and genuine. "Fair enough. How is boarding school? Are you making new friends?"

She didn't mention all of those stupid letters she'd written to him, detailing her friends and the various adventures they had, sneaking out late at night to talk and laugh, or studying late into the night for exams. "It's cold," she admitted, turning to look at the guests mingling in the warm light of the ballroom. "I'm not a huge fan of Switzerland."

He laughed. "What's not to love? The mixed languages? The massive mountains? The beauty of the trees?"

"The freezing temperatures," she corrected with a sardonic look up at him. "The mean headmistress who prefers to start the day with profound quotes from famous people that we are required to memorize each day. The lack of cell phones. The grey uniforms. Endless chores, boring food, intense classes, and seemingly endless homework?"

She noticed his dark eyebrows lift in mock surprise. "Yikes! No cell phones? How do you communicate with your friends at home?"

She snorted. "I know you're teasing me, but why don't you try living without a cell phone for just twenty-four hours and then mock me."

He chuckled, nodding his head. "Fair enough. I like being connected to the world, so I could see that being a problem. Especially for teenage girls who want to gossip without a teacher or headmistress overhearing."

"Exactly," she replied, smiling to show him that she wasn't bothered by his stereotyping of her needing to gossip with her friends. A moment later, she lowered her head, pulling at the pretty, pink ribbon wrapped around the small present. "What is it?" she asked.

Rian shrugged with a challenging smile. "Open it and see."

Amilee debated opening the box versus savoring the anticipation a little longer. In the end, she wanted to see what he'd chosen for her. She remembered how thoughtful he'd been at their betrothal ceremony. Several times over the past two years, she'd thought about their kitchen raid and how much fun it had been to sit with him and talk. Perhaps it had only been her imagination, or maybe Amilee was resentful of the way no one listened to her now, but those memories of being with him, talking with him and really being "heard" had helped her through the cold, lonely years at boarding school.

"Okay, I'll open it," she told him, trying to tamp down on her excitement. She wanted him to perceive her as sophisticated and womanly, but she suspected that some of her childish eagerness seeped through.

"Are you even going to give me a hint?" she asked as she tugged at the lovely ribbon.

"Not a chance," he replied with a soft laugh. "You'll see it in a moment."

Amilee ripped the paper and pulled out the box. She glanced at him, realized that he was peering over her shoulder and her heart thudded painfully against her ribs, although she didn't fully understand why.

Focusing on the box, Amilee carefully lifted the lid, staring down at a beautiful silver locket. "Oh, how lovely!" she gasped, lifting it up to examine it in the reflected moonlight. "How did...?" she started, only to stop at the odd look in his eyes.

Amilee realized he was seeing the locket for the first time as well, and the fact that he hadn't chosen the present significantly dimmed her pleasure.

Lowering the necklace to her lap, she carefully tucked it back into the wooden box. "Thank you," she finally replied, wishing that her voice wasn't so stiffly formal, but the pain ricocheting around inside of her was hard to suppress. "It's lovely." She tried desperately not to let the disappointment show on her features, forcing her lips into a polite smile, just as her mother had taught her.

Perhaps she wasn't as good at her hiding her emotions as she should be, because Amilee saw something flash in his eyes. But the emotion was quickly hidden. "Would you like help putting it on?" he offered.

Amilee shrugged and set the package off to the side. "That would be nice." Their conversation was suddenly so formal!

"Here," he said, taking up the necklace. "Turn around."

Amilee turned, giving him her back. While he fiddled with the clasp, Amilee peeked over her shoulder at him, trying to find a conversational topic that would allow her to hide her pain.

"So, you finished college?"

"Yes," he replied, obviously distracted. He lifted the necklace over her head. "But I'll continue with graduate school next year."

Amilee smiled and, for a brief moment, his arms surrounded her. For that instant, Amilee pretended that this man was truly hers. The feeling of his arms around her warmed her right down to her toes. She closed her eyes and pretended, savoring this moment for the future when she might allow herself to believe that...that...that she was important to him. That she mattered.

Then his arms disappeared. He adjusted the clasp, and she turned around, facing him once again.

Rian rested one arm against the back of the bench now as he asked casually, "Are you dating anyone at school?"

That certainly dashed her schoolgirl fantasies! A guy who cared about a girl definitely didn't encourage her to see other men!

She schooled her features into a placid expression. "No. I'm definitely not seeing anyone special."

A night bird trilled as the cicadas sang their usual song. "Why not?" he asked, turning slightly to face the courtyard again.

She laughed self-consciously and gazed out at the white flowers reaching up into the moonlight. "Because everyone at school knows that I'm betrothed." She shot him a sideways look. "You're kind of a rock star among my classmates."

He chuckled and, for some strange reason, a shiver of awareness drifted through her. "Is that so?"

"Absolutely," she teased. "There are posters of you. And some of my classmates put on lipstick and kiss your picture."

His eyes flashed back to her, a horrified look on his ruggedly handsome features. "Are you kidding?"

"Yes!" she replied, laughing.

He heaved a sigh of relief and she laughed again, leaning back against the bench. "But they are jealous that I'm betrothed to you. They ask me all sorts of questions about you."

"What kinds of questions?"

She pretended to think about it, when in reality, she knew all of the questions by heart because she'd had to make up answers so she didn't appear pathetic. It was seriously embarrassing to be betrothed to a man and not even know his favorite color.

"Well, they ask me what you like to eat, how tall you are, what your favorite color is, what you do in your spare time." She shrugged.

"What do you tell them?" he asked, resting his arm against the back of the bench.

"I tell them that you don't eat meat. That you're about five feet, two inches tall, but you look taller because the reporters are usually in the audience so the angle of their pictures supports my answer." She ignored his grunt of horror. "Your favorite colors are shell pink and baby blue and your favorite pastime is spanking women."

Amilee shifted slightly, fighting not to laugh at his horrified expression.

"Where did you...I don't...!" he sputtered.

She giggled, then slapped her hand over her mouth.

Rian looked at her, realized that she was teasing him and groaned.

"You're a brat," he blurted, laughing at her outrageousness. "The only woman I'm going to spank is *you!*"

Amilee laughed again, delighted that he felt comfortable enough to tease her back.

"I guess I should apologize, shouldn't I?" Amilee smoothed a hand down over the royal blue material of her dress. It wasn't quite a sheath dress, but it was about as close to one as a fourteen year old without discernable boobs could manage. This dress wasn't as ridiculous as the last one he'd seen her in. That ruffled monstrosity had been stuffed into the back of her closet after that betrothal event, never to be seen again.

"Don't bother. I won't believe you," he grumbled. He paused for a moment, chuckled, then changed the subject. "How are your classes?" he asked.

She shrugged, pretending that she hadn't mailed him detailed descriptions of her classes, teachers, and the regimen of homework every month. Letters he obviously hadn't read. "They are fine. I'm learning French and German this year. I enjoy languages."

A scuffling echoed through the peace of the courtyard. With sadness and aching disappointment, Amilee watched as the group of friends he'd introduced her to two years ago, laughed as they pulled out cigarettes, lighting up and taking their first, deep drag before blowing the smoke up into the air above them. They hadn't been at her birthday dinner, so when had they arrived?

Pain and disappointment washed over her as the laughing, gregarious, and ultra-sophisticated group moved down the long pathway opposite the ballroom. At the moment, none had noticed she and Rian were out here, watching them. "Your friends are looking for you," she murmured as one of the women pulled out a cell phone and dialed a number. A moment later, Rian's cell phone rang.

"They can wait."

Amilee closed the wooden box and smiled at him, again, hiding her emotions behind the polite smile that hurt her cheeks. "You know they won't stop."

He groaned as the phone rang again. He pulled the phone out of his pocket and frowned down at the screen, rubbing a hand over his face. In frustration?

"I'll just go tell them that we'll head out later."

He started to stand up, but Amilee put a hand on his and he froze. "Go ahead," she stated firmly. "I'm fourteen years old and you don't have to hang out with me."

He shook his head, gesturing to the threesome stepping through the glass doors, heading towards the library. They knew where the good booze was kept and made a beeline for the liquor cabinet. "Amilee, I just…"

She smiled up at him. "Go ahead, Your Highness. I'm heading back inside." Her dimples appeared and she laughed softly. "It's probably past my bed time."

He laughed as well, just as she'd hoped he would, and then he bent down and kissed her forehead. "Until the next time we meet, then."

A moment later, he was gone and she watched from the courtyard as he greeted his friends. But he must have known that she was still out here because Rian hurried them away from the windows, closing the doors to the library, so their antics couldn't be observed. What he didn't realize was that he then herded them into the billiards room, which was just off the library. With the lights on, she could still see everything.

Rian leaned a shoulder against the wall, wishing that he'd followed his instincts and gotten Amilee the book on women's history for her birthday. The locket his father's assistant had selected was pretty, but it seemed so impersonal. Amilee deserved better.

Roger walked up, sipping a glass of whatever he'd found behind the bar. "How's your little fiancée? Is she in bed now?" he asked with a snort of derisive laughter.

Rian looked down at the shorter man, disgusted with him all of a sudden. "If you are referring to Amilee, then I'd appreciate it if you'd show her a little respect."

Roger understood the angry tone and lifted his hands in mock surrender, although he clearly wasn't repentant. "Sorry. I didn't know that you were so protective of the child."

Even those words rankled, because Amilee might be only fourteen, but she was smart and funny and insightful. Hell, she was a whole lot more observant than all of these idiots put together.

Which begged the question, *why* had he invited them here tonight? He looked around, wondering why he was friends with these people. But was he really friends with them? Or were they here simply because they had nothing better to do? They had no goals in life, no purpose other than to find the next activity that may or may not amuse them.

Now that he was really seeing them, really understanding their personalities, it sickened him that he was one of them. What was he doing? He had about a million things to do, vital contracts to review and important decisions to make. His father was dying, and it was time for Rian to start to take on more of the leadership responsibilities. The cancer was slowly eating away at his father's pancreas. They'd hidden it from the world thus far, but soon they wouldn't be able to hide the ravages the disease was making on the man's body.

Still, Rian didn't want to take anything away from his father that he wasn't willing to relinquish. If his father wanted to continue to work, then Rian wasn't going to stop him. But it was time to have that conversation.

"Earth to Rian!" Razeem called out, snapping her fingers in his face.

He jerked back to the present, blinking down at her. Her ruby red lips curled into what she probably thought of as a seductive smile, the invitation in her eyes obvious. Rian remembered Amilee's words the first time she'd met his friends, that Razeen wanted him. Despite their previous intimate encounter, the idea of a repeat performance with Razeen repulsed him. Now he wondered why he'd given in to her in the first place. Razeen was another hanger-on that had no purpose. No goals and no desire to have anything other than a good time.

Even Amilee, a fourteen year old whose life was already mapped out for her, had found a passion; women's history. That couldn't be said for his friends. They had no passion other than finding the next party or night club.

"I have to go," he announced, placing the pool stick back in the holder. "I won't be joining you tomorrow. I have work I need to finish." And he walked out, feeling foolish for not seeing something that even Amilee had comprehended on her first meeting with them.

Chapter 3

Six Years Later...

Rian stared at the woman walking into the ballroom, stunned and... angry? No, not angry, but definitely stunned and...well, stunned! He couldn't find another word for what he was feeling now.

Betrayed? Yes, that term was certainly applicable. He definitely felt betrayed. Whether that was a legitimate emotion, he didn't give a damn. Seeing Amilee, her soft, feminine form wrapped up in a shimmering cocktail dress of cornflower blue that enhanced her creamy complexion and seemed to heighten the lovely sheen in her dark hair... then there was her graceful movements and the lovely smile she bestowed on...some ass that didn't deserve her smile!

Rian wanted to...!

"Your Highness?" Rual, his assistant asked, standing almost directly behind him. No one could enter the ballroom since Rian stood in the doorway, glowering at the woman who was supposed to be his wife! She was twenty years old now. Twenty! He could have married her two years ago! But he'd waited, wanting her to enjoy college life a bit longer. Rian had told himself that Amilee deserved a bit more freedom before she was trapped into married life with him and all of the constrictions of palace life.

But when had she become this ravishing beauty? When had her pretty features morphed into...shocking loveliness?!

And why the hell was he so angry? His pretty betrothed had transformed into a stunning woman! He should be happy!

"Your Highness!" Rual hissed.

Rian angrily glanced at his assistant, wondering what the hell was wrong with him!

"Everyone is staring!" Rual explained in a low whisper.

Rian looked around. Sure enough, several of the guests were smiling at him as he glared at his fiancée.

"Right," he muttered, along with several curses that he kept to himself.

He started to move forward, but suddenly realized that his body was…aroused? What the hell?!

Unfortunately, that was the moment that the guests realized that he'd entered the ballroom. A silence descended over the room and, for the first time in his life, he felt self-conscious about the attention directed at him. All his life, he'd accepted that people would stare and talk, agree and disagree with his policies. They would whisper and speculate, gossip and comment about any and everything about his life. But at this moment, he wanted everyone to just…disappear so that he could deal with the reality of this moment.

He was attracted to his fiancée!

No "attraction" was too tame of a word for what he felt. He wanted to pull her into his arms and explore every soft, voluptuous curve. He wanted to kiss her and explore the soft lips, to press her body against his and discover what she felt like. And yet, he also wanted to simply stand here and admire her. To take in every delectable curve on her body. Had she known how that dress would cling to her lovely curves?

Of course she did! Every woman knew the tricks that brought a man to his knees! But this woman…Amilee was better than most. It wasn't that she was simply alluring and enticing. There was an aura of innocence around her. It was almost as if there was a glittering neon sign over her head that flashed, "You can look, but you can't have!" For a man like Rian, that challenge was like waving a red flag in front of a bull. He wanted to charge. He wanted to walk over to her, pick her up, and carry her out of here!

Damn it! How many years had the palace staff organized a birthday celebration for Amilee? How many times had he spoken to her, smiled down into her innocent eyes? But now…there would be no smiling. Not tonight! Tonight, he wanted to take her away and make love to her!

How the hell had that happened? How had she turned into this woman, this alluring, tempting creature, without his knowledge?

The orchestra started playing a new song, something that startled him enough that he snapped out of his contemplation of Amilee. Looking away, he surveyed the other guests, forcing his feet to carry him further into the room. The overhead lights shimmered upon the guests while a small orchestra played off to the left. The ballroom was covered in gold leaf with the colors of Abidnae in the furniture, flags, and uniforms of the servants. Even the marble floor was embellished with the seal of

Abidnae. The elegance of the room normally overwhelmed the guests. But this time, the beauty of Amilee overwhelmed Rian.

He nodded at several people but didn't recognize anyone, still focused on Amilee's transformation. To be more specific, he was contemplating bending her over his knee and spanking her!

For becoming the stunning beauty he'd foreseen years ago? That was ludicrous. But yes, that was exactly what he was angry about. Furious, even.

He stopped and spoke to several people, but his every thought was focused on her. He knew the exact moment she moved, where she went, whom she spoke with, and…yes, he knew when she decided to slip out the door. It was almost as if he could read her mind.

Circumventing her escape, Rian shifted his route so he could intersect her path. It was almost amusing, this game of cat and mouse. Plus, her attempts to allude him put him back in control. He was the predator and Amilee, the prey!

Closer and closer, he stalked through the room, stopping to speak with one person, greeting another with a short handshake. Relentlessly, he moved towards her, amused by her futile attempts to outmaneuver him.

"I'm sorry, Mr. Caligari," he heard Amilee say, "but I need to slip out for…"

"Amilee."

One word. Just one word and she felt as if she might melt into a puddle at his feet! What magic was this? What sorcery?

Amilee trembled as Rian, Sheik Rian now, stepped closer, taking her hands in his own.

"Your Highness," she whispered through suddenly numb lips as she stared at the collar of her betrothed. Protocol demanded that she look into his eyes, but that was impossible! No way could she…!

His thumb brushed against her pulse, the touch so startling that she gasped!

"You were saying?" he prompted, his voice low. Husky. His eyes dark and penetrating as she looked up at him, wishing she could remember why she didn't want this! Because right now, she wanted nothing more than to stare into his eyes forever. How many years had she been engaged to him? How long had she known that this man would someday become her husband? But never, not in all this time, had she suspected that she would react this way! Her reaction was completely irrational and yet, she couldn't seem to look away.

Rian turned, tucking her hand onto the crook of his arm. The movement brought her closer and Amilee could feel the warmth of him under her hand, her fingertips finding the muscles hidden underneath his jacket.

"You look lovely tonight," he commented, nodding to one of his cabinet members. Amilee understood her place and she smiled to the man as well, acknowledging each person moments after Rian. Because this protocol had been drilled into her over the years, she knew her role and did it extremely well, even if a part of her rebelled at acknowledging someone only after Rian had done so. She wasn't a shadow, she told herself, but at the moment, she was too…overwhelmed to do anything more.

"Thank you, Your Highness." She bit her lip, trying to remember what was expected of her next. "Thank you for another lovely birthday party." Even though none of *her* friends had been invited, she thought resentfully. They continued to walk through the crowds, Rian still nodding and Amilee walking stiffly beside him. Surely everyone who looked at them grasped the strained silence between them, didn't they?

"You're welcome," he replied, his voice husky but still polite. "You're twenty now, correct?"

"Yes. Twenty years old." When she had a modicum of control back, Amilee looked up at him and was startled by the flash of…what? Amilee didn't care! No matter what was going through his mind, she wasn't ready!

Turning, she pulled her hand away and stood in front of him, unaware of how her chin lifted or the way her eyes flashed with her determination. She had to get this out before…before he decreed that they would marry! "I want to finish my degree, Your Highness."

Amilee's long, dark lashes lowered and he felt like roaring with frustration. But then she looked up at him through those lashes and his body reacted with an intensity that astounded him!

"You have your degree, don't you, Your Highness?" she asked. "In fact, I believe you went on to earn a Master's in economics and business, didn't you?"

His eyes narrowed and that spanking was becoming more imminent. "Yes."

Amilee looked away, then brought her eyes right back to his. "I want to finish my degree, Your Highness. I don't think there's any reason to rush into a marriage when neither of us are truly prepared for what we will face in the future."

Rian considered the possible future, much of which included a bed with Amilee naked while he explored every inch of her delectable body!

"What would prepare us?" he asked, nodding to the events coordinator when she gave the signal that dinner was ready. He took Amilee's hand, placing it on his elbow, leading her towards the dining room.

"A formal, *complete* education, Your Highness," she stated firmly.

Rian pulled out her chair, waiting until she sat down before taking his seat. The other guests quickly moved into the room and found their assigned table, sitting down amid a flurry of conversation.

"In other words, you want to delay our wedding until after you've finished college," he said, his irritation ramping up even higher.

"Yes, Your Highness," she replied.

The other guest assigned to their table joined them. "We'll continue this conversation later," he said as she drew a breath to argue her point further. "In private."

Over the course of the meal, Rian watched Amilee carefully, impressed with her manners and the easy way she conversed with everyone at the table. She chose topics that were sure to include everyone, but nothing controversial. No need to start a major political battle over a meal, he thought.

He enjoyed watching Amilee eat. Gone was the child who had learned to mimic adult manners and conversation. In her place was a graceful woman with an easy, natural demeanor. In addition, she was able to converse intelligently about every topic brought up. Her smiles were easy and genuine even if her posture was a bit stiff and...what was it about the way she was sitting in her chair? She was...tense? It didn't show in the way she spoke. She had everyone laughing.

Testing out a theory, he moved his arm, resting his hand on the back of her chair. The movement came across to the other guests as territorial, but none seemed to mind since the two of them had been betrothed for the better part of a decade.

But as soon as he moved his arm, Amilee dropped her fork, the clatter resounding around the table. She smoothly apologized to the others and continued the conversation, but the slip was...interesting!

Suddenly, Rian felt significantly better about the night. Amilee was just as affected by his presence as he was by her! He could feel the tension vibrating off her, noticed the slight blush to her creamy complexion. Interesting, he thought.

At the end of the meal, the orchestra started up again. Rian was the first to stand and he extended his hand towards Amilee. "Will you do me the honor of this dance?" he asked formally.

Even as he watched, he noticed that she stopped breathing, her gaze going to his hand, then up to look him in the eyes. The pleading was there, but Rian didn't relent. He couldn't. Touching her, holding this woman in his arms was imperative. He needed to know, needed to confirm his suspicions.

"Come," he urged, taking her hand and leading her out of the dining room and back into the ballroom. "Did you enjoy your birthday dinner?" he asked softly, wanting to nuzzle the delicate skin of her throat. He didn't, but only because everyone was watching them now.

"Yes, it was lovely," she replied, staring at something over his shoulder.

"Aren't you interested in opening my present?"

Amilee was startled and looked up into his dark eyes, praying that he couldn't see the need in her own, or feel how she was trembling. He was too close. She wished that tonight hadn't included dancing! Darn it, this was…it was all too much!

"Another piece of jewelry, Your Highness?" she asked, thinking back to the other pieces that he'd gifted her on other birthdays. The locket had been banished to the back of her jewelry case, never worn again after that night. Not that Rian would care, she told herself. He probably had forgotten that he'd given it to her. Just as he'd probably forgotten the pearl necklace, pearl earrings, and other assorted jewelry that he'd given to her over the years. Suspecting that he hadn't selected any of them, Amilee hadn't felt guilty by not wearing them.

"You'll have to wait and see." He spun her around, pulling her in closer so that she was now pressed against him. Amilee closed her eyes, trying not to react. But the soft laughter in her ear warned her that Rian was a bit more perceptive. At least he was perceptive when it came to things of a sexual nature, she thought. Other issues, he was a bit more oblivious.

"Why don't we go out to the courtyard where you can open my present in private?" he offered.

Amilee looked around, startled to discover that the other guests were dancing around them. In her mind, they were alone in an intimate bubble.

Several of the older couples smiled in a knowing way that caused Amilee to wonder if she'd done something…revealing…during the moments in Rian's arms. She didn't like to think so, but…she'd been a bit overwhelmed by the man.

"Yes. Fine. I'll open your present," she replied, wanting to get away from all of the eyes that were now watching her and Rian. "But not here. Not while everyone is watching." She turned her head slightly, looking at the knot of his dark tie. "We could do it outside. The courtyard would be nice. It's probably cooled down by now."

Rian took her hand in his, but this time, he didn't place her hand on his arm. Instead, he continued to hold her fingers loosely in his hand.

She wondered what he would do if she pulled away, but one glance at her mother's stern approval told Amilee to wait until they were alone.

As soon as the darkness surrounded them, Amilee knew that this had been a mistake. She shouldn't be out here alone with Rian! There was a new moon, so it was dark tonight. It was...too intimate!

"Let's go sit on our bench," he suggested.

No, she thought frantically. Not that bench! "Maybe we should go back inside," she offered. "It seems a bit rude to leave the party."

Rian laughed softly, tugging her along the pathway. "I don't think anyone will miss us. At least for a few moments while you unwrap your present."

With a sigh, Amilee sat down on the bench, glanced through the windows, then to Rian as he sat down next to her. "Where are your friends?" she asked, wishing that they were here, that they would take Rian away so she didn't feel this...crazy, breathless sensation. She didn't want to be attracted to Rian! She preferred the indifference towards him that she convinced herself that she felt for him whenever they were apart!

"They are skiing in Italy, I believe. Or maybe they're out to sea, partying." He put a beautifully wrapped present on her lap. "They aren't my concern tonight," he told her.

Oh, how those words thrilled her! How many nights had she sat here, looking through the windows at the others and at him, wishing that she were important to him? How many times had she watched him walk away with his friends or his advisors because, whatever they needed, those activities were more important?

Too often, she answered her own question. So now she was sitting here, getting exactly what she'd dreamed of. Why was she being such a ninny?! Why couldn't she just...accept this moment?

Because she didn't trust it. Or maybe she didn't trust herself.

"Savoring the anticipation, Amilee?" he teased.

Amilee looked up at him, startled by his teasing. She hadn't been savoring anything, but it was as good of an excuse as anything. She forced her lips into a smile as her fingers plucked at the sparkly ribbon that bound the present. "You know how much I enjoy the anticipation, Your Highness," she said, forcing a laugh.

"I remember. I've learned a few things about you over the years," he replied, amusement coloring his tone.

Amilee laughed again, but it was genuine this time. "Well, I guess I should get to it," she said, but her fingers still toyed with the paper and the ribbon, not wanting to let this moment go. Ever since they'd pilfered treats from the kitchen that first time, she'd wanted his undivided attention. Now that she had it, she didn't want to give it up.

"What do you think it is?" he asked, leaning back and extending his arm along the back of the bench.

She shrugged slightly. "You've given me jewelry every year for my birthday since the first time we met, Your Highness. So, I'm assuming that this is another piece of jewelry."

"I suspect that you have enough pearls," he replied dryly. His eyes dropped to her fingers, plucking at the wrapping paper, then up into her chocolate eyes, daring her. "You're going to have to open it at some point."

Amilee sighed. "Yes. I suppose so." Slowly, she tore at the wrapping paper, hoping that this was something other than jewelry. The sparkling paper revealed a wooden box. Hope plummeted, the disappointment leaving a metallic taste in her mouth. More jewelry.

"Thank you," she whispered, fighting back the stab of disappointment.

"Open the box, Amilee," he urged softly.

Slowly, her fingers fiddling unsteadily with the latch on the lovely box, she lifted the lid and…!

"What is this?" she whispered, staring down at the book inside the box. It definitely wasn't jewelry!

"I was in Spain two months ago and found this," he explained, reverently lifting the book out of the box. The papers were old and crinkled, the front cover no longer attached. "I thought that you might find it interesting. It's the–"

"Examen de Ingenios!" she interrupted in a reverent whisper. "Written in 1616! It's beautiful!"

"You like it?"

She glanced briefly up at him, before her eyes returned to the ancient book. "I love it!" she gasped. "The author, Juan Huarte, wrote about how each person's personality could thrive doing specific kinds of work." She ran gentle fingers over the front cover, before quickly pulling her hands away. "We shouldn't be touching this with our bare hands. We should be wearing cotton gloves. The oils from our fingers will deteriorate the pages!"

Rian nodded. "Yes, but I thought that, this first time, you should see it without gloves."

Amilee could barely breathe, not just because of the thoughtful, beautiful gift, but also because…well, because she was touched. This gift, it was personal! He knew she was studying psychology and he'd thought of her! Of course, he might have still staffed out the purchase of the book, but he'd clearly put thought into what she might like.

"It's beautiful," she whispered, running a worshipful finger over the cover. Beaming up at him, she blinked back tears. "Thank you."

And...at that same moment, his seemingly ever-present aid stepped out of the shadows, bowing as he stood about three feet away.

"I apologize, Your Highness, but the phone call you were waiting on..."

There was a tense, pregnant moment...a moment when time seemed to stand still. There was no music seeping from the ballroom, no aide standing silently off to the side. There was just the moonlight, Rian and Amilee, the tension pulsing through the air between them. It was ripe for hope, for hope in the future, and the potential for...something more. Something that neither of them dared to speak or think. It throbbed between them.

Then his aide shifted with a hint of impatience and the moment ended. The pulsing diminished and Rian looked away. "Right," Rian sighed. He looked apologetically at Amilee. "I'm so sorry to cut our time together short, again. I promise that it won't be this hectic after our wedding. I'll ensure that our honeymoon is unbroken by..."

"We can't!" she gasped, standing up at the same time he did. Rian stopped and blinked down at her.

"We can't...what?" he asked.

"Marry!"

He laughed, taking her hand in his, lifting her fingers to his lips. "I'm afraid we must."

"But..." her mind blanked at the touch of his lips on her fingers. She wanted to pull her hand away, but at the same time, she wanted to move closer, to ask that he truly kiss her.

"But you want to finish your degree," he finished for her. With a sigh, he tucked her hand onto his arm as he led her out of the courtyard. "How about a compromise?" he offered.

"What sort of compromise, Your Highness?" she asked, wary but intrigued.

"You will call me Rian instead of 'Your Highness'."

"I can do that!" she agreed, eager to grab onto any delay in marriage that she could. Nothing made sense when he was around and she needed her world to make sense!

"And," he continued, still walking along the pathway, but obviously in no hurry to get to that phone call, "you and I will converse throughout the year. Actually, I'd prefer that we converse on the phone and not through those stilted, formal letters that your mother insists on." He stopped and smiled down at her. "In the past, we've met only on your birthdays. That leaves too many days between our meetings, during which time, we could be getting to know each other so that we can start to build a strong marriage."

That seemed very fair, but…what was the catch? "I can e-mail you," she told him. For a moment, she bit her lip, contemplating his offer and trying to come up with ways to implement his request. "I know that I've been writing you letters and, you guess correctly that my mother requires me to write them. I know they aren't very personal but… how about if we email each other instead? Email is much faster and I can send you messages about what's happening in my life whenever something interesting happens." She hated writing letters. Her mother demanded that she hand write the letters, but after being in college for the past two years, she'd become a very fast typist.

He paused to consider her offer. "You will ask questions and answer mine?" he asked.

"Yes!" she gasped, desperate to do anything that might delay a wedding to a man who was basically a stranger, despite the fact that they'd been betrothed for eight years.

"Fine," he replied, releasing her hand as he bowed slightly. "It's a deal."

With that, he walked away, leaving Amilee both giddy with excitement over the delay, but also…confused? Elated? Yes. And…there was a sensation of being let down that she hadn't expected. Odd, she thought as she turned and returned to the bench. Reverently, she picked up the book, smiling as she let her finger caress the cover one more time. Relieved, she walked to the other side of the courtyard, not wanting to go back to "her" party.

Chapter 4

Two years later...

Amilee watched as he approached, trying to hide her trembling anticipation. "Be sophisticated," she admonished herself. "He's a sheik! Don't be a ninny!"

The words echoed through her mind as she watched the man walk through the dark garden. There was no hesitation in his step. The man must have eyes like a cat, she thought, because he never slowed to navigate the complicated pathways or low hanging trees. And his eyes never strayed from this spot she'd selected.

"You came," he said, his voice deep and husky as he stepped closer to her.

"You asked me to." Was her voice a bit too breathless? Sophisticated, she admonished herself mentally.

"Yes, but I wasn't sure if you'd dare," he replied, stepping closer still, reaching out to slide a hand along her waist. "I thought that our emails over the past several weeks might have put me in the 'friend zone', which is why I asked you here."

Amilee couldn't stop the laugh from bursting from her. "I doubt that any woman with blood flowing through her veins could friend-zone you, Your Highness."

He inched even closer and she could feel the heat of his body against hers. "I thought you were going to call me Rian."

His voice lowered and Amilee shivered at the intimacy she heard in his tone. He must have felt the tremor because he pulled her closer, her breasts and stomach soft against the hardness of his chest and... goodness, she blushed as she realized what else was pressed against her. Thankfully, the darkness of the garden hid her blushing reaction, even as her body shifted against him, craving more contact. Her shyness seemed to melt away now as her need and greed to feel more of him swelled inside of her. She wanted him to kiss her, to feel his lips against hers, and to know the taste of him. But he was too tall and she wasn't that brave. Not yet.

"I remember," she replied.

"Say it," he urged, running his fingers through her hair. "Please, Amilee, say my name."

Could he possibly feel the same need and desire for her?

"Rian," she replied softly.

And then he kissed her. His mouth was soft and tender as he kissed her. But that wasn't what she wanted. Going up on her toes, she took and demanded and he responded by deepening the kiss, pulling her firmly against him, one hand tangling in her hair to tilt her head back so that he could kiss her more thoroughly. The darkness hid them, silently providing protection from the palace guests in the dining room and Amilee's heart pounded with feelings and sensations that threatened to overwhelm her.

Too soon, he pulled back, but didn't release her. Wrapped tightly in his arms, she felt cherished. Protected and almost ...loved? No, that was impossible. They might have known each other for years, but they didn't really "know" one another. Their real acquaintance, their email correspondence over the past several months was too new for an emotion that deep. She loved conversing with Rian via email, loved arguing with him, and debating the merits of books, politics, and current events. Over the past several weeks, she'd emailed Rian almost every day and had enjoyed every conversation fully. More than she wanted to admit, even to herself.

But love? No. It was too soon for love. That was just a silly, girlish fantasy. Love at first sight wasn't real. So what she was feeling now, was just...infatuation.

And yet, she snuggled closer, feeling him press a kiss to the top of her head and Amilee smiled at the sweetness of it all. She never would have thought that a man as terrifyingly intimidating, even predatory as he walked into any room or down a hallway, could be this sweet and gentle.

"We need to go back inside," he grumbled reluctantly, clearly unwilling to break the tenuous moment.

Amilee knew he was right. Being alone together like this would give the matrons something to gossip about. Even though Amilee was in her last year of undergrad studies, she still didn't like to be included in the wonderings of others. It might sully what was happening between herself and Rian, and it would also affect her father's role in the Abidnae government. That was something she wouldn't allow to happen.

"You're right," she whispered back. Slowly, their arms loosened from each other and she stepped back, gazing up into his dark eyes. "I will–"

"Do this again," he finished for her.

Amilee laughed. "I certainly hope so."

Rian stepped back, taking her hand. "Classes start again in a few weeks, correct?"

"Yes. Three weeks," she replied, smiling when he lifted her fingers and kissed them softly. "I only have two more semesters, then I'll have my degree."

"That's quite an accomplishment." They turned the corner and he dropped her hand. "Will you have lunch with me tomorrow?"

She tilted her head. "I didn't know that my father–"

"Not with your father, Amilee," he interrupted. "Just you and me."

The significance of his request hung in the darkness, pulsing with meaning. "Yes," she whispered.

His response was to bend down and brush his lips against hers. Just briefly, before he pulled away with a gentle squeeze of her hand. "Go," he urged. "I told the group that I had to take a phone call, so I'll come in from the other door."

She smiled, appreciating his discretion and understanding of how vicious the gossips could be. It was a dinner with some of his advisors and their wives, but she still didn't want anyone to know about....well, whatever was happening between them. The press would hound her and her father, demanding to know when the long-anticipated wedding was to take place. Discretion was his whole world and she watched as he moved towards the opposite doorway.

When she stepped back into the palace, Amilee blinked at the bright lights as well as the cacophony of sounds. Coming from the quiet darkness of the gardens into this onslaught of conversation was a bit startling.

"Are you okay?"

Amilee looked at her father and smiled. "Of course. Why?"

"You look a bit flushed," he replied, wrapping an arm protectively around her waist. "I'm ready to head out. Unless you'd like to stay longer?" he asked, his eyes narrowing as he watched Rian walk into the room from the opposite doorway. Her father wasn't a fool, Amilee knew. Far from it, which was why he was so good at his job. As director of the intelligence agency for Abidnae, he was the highest ranking official outside of Rian's advisory council. Hiding her reaction, she ducked her head and nodded. "Yes. It's definitely time to go home."

But as she lifted her head, a woman...the woman she'd seen several times over the years, draped her body against Rian's and slid her hands up his chest, resting them on his shoulders. Amilee was stunned, shocked at how perfectly Rian and Razeen fit together. They looked… right. Razeen was tall, painfully thin, and stunningly beautiful. Amilee had disliked Razeen ever since that damnable betrothal ceremony. That dislike had bloomed into outright hatred over time.

Amilee had never hated anyone as much as she did that woman with her icky red lips and her reed-thin body pressed against Rian.

Unfortunately, this wasn't one of the sweet, tender kisses that she'd shared with Rian just minutes ago. No, this was…this kiss was more. So much more!

With a gasp, Amilee turned away, hurt and shocked. She'd just been in Rian's arms, felt the magic of his kiss but…it hadn't been magical! The magic had only been in her head. Her response had merely been her reaction to the man's extensive experience at kissing!

The ache in her chest was almost too much to endure, but Amilee lifted her head and blinked back tears as she hurried ahead of her father through the elaborate hallways of the palace. Thankfully, his driver was waiting outside with the doors of his town car open, allowing Amilee to dive into the darkened back seat. Her father was already on the phone, she had no idea who with, nor did she care. Amilee stared out the window, refusing to cry. She wouldn't let this hurt! Not by a man who could…well, it didn't matter! Not anymore!

And lunch tomorrow? Alone with a man who could kiss her so sweetly one moment, then go straight into the arms of another woman? No. Absolutely not. She'd send her regrets as soon as she got home tonight

Chapter 5

Two years later...

Amilee stared at her reflection in the mirror. Taking a deep breath, she smoothed a hand nervously down her stomach. She hadn't seen Rian in two years! Ever since her twenty-second birthday, when she'd seen Rian kissing Razeen, Amilee had found excuses to be absent for her birthday. Unfortunately, her parents had demanded that nothing get in the way of a birthday celebration this year. What was so special about this year? She was twenty-four and "finished with college", at least, according to her mother.

In other words, her mother deemed her to be "of marriageable age" and commanded that Amilee present herself tonight. Amilee knew very well that this was an inspection. Amilee's mother was hoping that Sheik Rian would take one look at her and decide that it was time for marriage.

However, Amilee's hopes leaned in a different direction. She didn't want to marry Rian. Hence the dull, brown dress that did her complexion no favors. Plus, the shapeless design hid her figure, a figure that had matured over the years. Gone was the plain child and in her place was a woman who...okay, maybe she could stand to lose ten pounds. But Amilee felt pretty, even if she wanted to hide her changed appearance, if only for tonight. She'd also chosen kitten heels so that she was shorter than normal. Looking at herself, Amilee wondered if there was something else she could do to make herself appear undesirable.

Not that she had any hope of being remotely enticing to the man. She knew the women that Rian preferred. The lovely Razeen with her willowy figure popped into Amilee's mind. Yes, Razeen was the type of woman that Rian should marry, she thought. Razeen was beautiful and vibrant. She could wear all of the latest styles from Paris and wouldn't embarrass Rian. Amilee didn't have that option. Her figure was... curvy. Yes, that was the right description. Curvy in her hips and her breasts and her thighs...sighing, Amilee turned away from the mirror, picking up the stupid locket that Rian had given her so many years ago.

Her mother had ordered her to wear the locket tonight, but Amilee had never put a picture in it. So, what was the point? A locket was a keepsake piece. But Amilee had nothing to "keep".

"I hate this!" she hissed as she stalked out of her bedroom.

Twenty minutes later, she and her parents stepped into the elegant dining room of the Abidnae palace. Looking around, Amilee searched for Rian, wanting to get this initial confrontation over with. Of course, it wouldn't be a confrontation if she'd just...give in. Accept her fate.

As soon as those words filtered through her mind, Amilee rejected them. Lifting her chin, she hardened her resolve. Amilee couldn't accept being married to Rian. She simply wouldn't allow herself to be married to a man who...kissed other women. That wouldn't hurt so badly except that his kissing of Razeen happened only moments after he'd kissed Amilee. It had been her first kiss. Her first and only kiss!

Try as she might, Amilee couldn't seem to banish the image from her thoughts. Over the past two years, she'd focused all of her energy into her classes, studying for long hours to get the best grades and the best internship, then be the best damn intern the mental health clinic had ever seen! Amilee had been fantastic at her job! People had said she was hard working, thoughtful, and insightful!

Studying and her internship had been a balm to her wounded ego. After watching her betrothed kiss Razeen, Amilee had been devastated, but she'd gotten past it. She'd moved on! She'd earned her degree, even finishing at the top of her class!

And yet, she could still feel the pain slicing through her as she'd watched the ever-so-beautiful-and-slender Razeen drape herself against Rian's tall, muscular body. Razeen had done exactly what Amilee had wanted to do, but couldn't.

Couldn't because she'd been too young at that point. Well, and too inexperienced to even know how to drape oneself against a man. Good grief, Amilee still had no idea how to do that. There was a grace to it, a fluidity that...well, Amilee simply wasn't a fluid person. She was soft and...fluffy. Yep, that was the right word. Fluffy. She was fluffy and curvy.

"Amilee!" Inis called out. "It is wonderful to see you again!"

Amilee smiled at the elderly woman who clasped both of her hands, holding them out to survey her outfit. The woman chuckled softly, shaking her head. "I see that you have a new plan in mind!"

Amilee felt her cheeks heating up, but tried to appear sophisticated. "Thank you for another lovely birthday dinner," she replied, unwilling to confirm or deny Rian's grandmother's suspicions regarding her choice of outfits.

"It's always a delight to celebrate this special day with you, my dear girl." Inis tucked Amilee's hand into her elbow, leading her into the family salon where they would enjoy a pre-dinner drink together. "And isn't it delightful that you are finally old enough to share a glass of wine with me!"

Amilee didn't bother to tell the woman that she'd shared many glasses of wine with her college friends over the years. Wine, beer, and a few spirits, although Amilee wasn't the kind who drank to excess. She'd never been one to enjoy losing control the way alcohol tended to do.

"It's very exciting," she replied politely.

Inis laughed, patting her hand. "Don't even try it, dear," she teased. "I know what happens at those college parties. And I sincerely hope that you've enjoyed your college years."

Was that an admonition towards her because she'd avoided this night for so long? She certainly hoped not. Amilee truly respected Inis. She'd been the one consistent friend whenever she'd visited the palace.

"I hope I haven't offended you by not being here. It's just–"

"Oh, heaven's child!" Inis interrupted Amilee's explanation. "No, you haven't offended me! In fact, I love that you have enjoyed yourself! You're young and you should be out doing things with other young people. Not coming here every year to endure the ordeal of..." She stopped as Rian walked into the room.

Tall and handsome, the sight of him took Amilee's breath away! Darn it, she wished that she could somehow grow out of this stupid, pointless reaction to the man!

Briefly, he scanned the room and Amilee could feel her heart accelerating, waiting and wondering if he might be looking for her.

When his eyes caught hers, everything else faded away. As always, Amilee had eyes only for Rian. With every step he took towards her, she felt her heart speed up. She hoped and prayed that he couldn't tell how excited she was to see him. Amilee desperately wanted to come across as unconcerned and casual. But the excitement of seeing him again after so long combined with the pain of that last image of him in another woman's arms...there was no way she could hide what she was feeling. Not anymore.

"Good evening, Amilee," he said, stopping in front of her and taking her free hand. "It is a delight to see you again after so many years."

Okay, that was definitely an admonition, she thought and pulled her hand away. Tilting her head slightly, she forced a smile. "I'm sure you understand how busy life can be, Your Highness?"

His eyes narrowed slightly but his lips quirked upwards at the corners. "Indeed I do. But I thought we'd agreed years ago that you were going to use my name."

Inis chuckled and stepped away. "You two battle this out. I'm getting a drink." And off she went, leaving Amilee to deal with him alone.

"Panicked?" he offered.

Amilee's eyes shot upwards. "Not at all, Your Highness," she replied, deliberately using the formal address.

"Ah, we're going to have to do something about this rebellion," he chuckled, taking her hand and tucking it onto his elbow. When Inis had done the same gesture, Amilee hadn't objected. But when Rian did it, she wanted to step back and...and...flee. But instead, she lifted her chin and walked towards one of the waiters alongside him.

"I have a favor to ask," she started out, determined to get this conversation over with.

"Anything at all, my dear." He took a glass of white wine, handing it to her as he reached for the crystal glass of scotch.

She held the glass of wine, not bothering to taste it. Not because she didn't want to drink the wine, but because she didn't want anything from this man. Not the wine, not the use of his name, and definitely not his wedding ring!

"I want to go to graduate school," she explained, her eyes revealing her determination as she lifted her gaze to glare up into his darker ones. "Just the fact that I'm asking permission to attend graduate school irritates me," she continued, ignoring the narrowing of his eyes. "But because we are," she sighed, hating the term, "betrothed..." she took another moment to calm her temper. "Because we are betrothed, I am essentially your property. So therefore, I have to ask your permission to continue my education." Amilee looked away, staring into the dark windows of the elegant room. "It's insulting and offensive, especially since you attended graduate school and I doubt you had to ask permission to continue your education." She looked at the other guests milling about the room, although she couldn't actually name anyone here tonight. Except her parents. And his parents.

After a prolonged silence, she realized that he hadn't answered her. Turning, she slowly lifted her eyes, trying to hide the anger simmering inside of her.

"Thank you."

Amilee blinked. "For what?"

"For finally acknowledging my presence," he snapped. "You've looked at every person in this room except me."

Her anger was forgotten for a brief moment as she realized that he appeared angry. But why?

"So, you want to attend graduate school."

"Yes," she replied quickly.

"And this means that you want to delay our wedding."

Amilee swallowed hard. "Yes."

"For how long?"

She opened her mouth, but tempered her response. "Never" wasn't a good answer. "I think it's only fair that I am allowed the same opportunities that you were permitted, Your Highness." She hid her smile when his lips compressed. "Do you not agree?"

Rian wanted to flip the beauty over his shoulder and spank her adorable bottom for her impudence. And no, he didn't agree that they should delay their wedding! He'd anticipated this night for months! He'd wanted to bed Amilee for years, but had held off, knowing that she was too young. And yes, even twenty-four seemed too young.

And yet, he couldn't deny her request. As much as he wanted her, and he could feel the attraction she felt for him as well, he wouldn't stop her from attaining her degree. It was such a simple request. Besides, it was entirely within her rights to obtain as much education as she wanted.

Unfortunately, that didn't bode well for him. Grinding his teeth, he nodded sharply. "Fine. Where did you plan to study?"

Joy lit up her eyes. Rian might have groaned at the image, but he was a bit too stunned.

"Since I wasn't sure if I'd be permitted to attend, I haven't investigated my options. But I'll let you know where I'm going as soon I have more information."

Damn, the delightful woman was literally vibrating with excitement. He wanted to hug her, pull her soft, delectable body close so that he could feel those lush curves against his body. Instead, he drained his glass of scotch. "I believe dinner is ready," he snapped. Immediately, a waiter stepped forward, taking his glass.

"Oh, how timely!" Amilee observed, handing the waiter her untouched glass of wine as she turned and headed towards the dining room. She didn't even wait for him, he thought in annoyance. The correct etiquette was for her to go into the dining room on his arm. Didn't she understand her place? Didn't she grasp the privilege that she was giving up by not walking into dinner on his arm?

"Good evening, darling!"

Rian sighed as Razeen appeared by his side. He fought not to cringe at her brittle tone as her hand with the red talons slid onto his arm. "Good evening, Razeen. You look lovely tonight, as always."

Razeen leaned forward, pressing her small, hard breasts against his upper arm. "You're always so charming, Your Highness," she said, laughing as she hugged his arm.

He didn't like her breasts, he thought. What in the world had attracted him to this woman all those years ago? And why did she continue to try to reignite that extinguished flame? There was no attraction between them now, at least, not from his side. Unfortunately, she just wouldn't give up. He might have disconnected with the old group of friends from college, but Razeen's father was one of his generals, so she accompanied him to the palace for various social functions. Sometimes even for the meetings. It was becoming annoying.

"How have you been lately, Razeen?" he asked politely, walking towards the dining room.

"Oh, you know, parties and fun," she said airily, waving a hand as if her lack of goals or ambitions was something to brag about.

"Are you working?"

She laughed as if he'd just asked a silly question. "Oh, goodness, Daddy would have a heart attack if I suggested getting a job! He likes knowing exactly where I am."

Her answer caused his eyes to move towards Amilee. He respected her ambitions a hell of a lot more than he respected Razeen's party attitude. Yes, life was short. But there was so much more to life than parties.

With Razeen's words, his anger and frustration towards Amilee diminished. Not his need for her. He still wanted to feel those soft, wonderful curves. He still wanted to explore every inch of her body and discover ways to turn her on. But he'd temper that need, since he liked the fact that she preferred education over flirtation.

"Your seat," he said to Razeen, wanting her away from him as quickly as possible.

"You're such a gentleman!" she replied, laughing up at him as he held her chair out for her. Once she was seated, he walked to the head of the table, sitting down next to Amilee who was already talking to the woman on her right. As she spoke, Rian watched, admiring her soft, sweet tones as well as the informed response to the man's questions about…hell, he had no idea.

Sighing, he resigned himself to more waiting. One more year, he thought. Two at the most. Yes, two years, and she'd finish her graduate work and he could finally claim his bride.

Chapter 6

Five damn years! Rian paced around Amilee's small office impatiently. He'd already scanned the titles on her bookshelf, perused the open calendar on her desk, and watched the traffic on the street down below. Granted, he'd arrived fifteen minutes prior to his "appointment", but he'd still expected Amilee to be here.

So, where the hell was she?!

Just as that furious thought popped into his mind, the door burst open and a harried Amilee rushed into the room. "I'm so sorry that I'm late!" she gushed. "I wasn't expecting my next client until..." she glanced down at her phone where she must have her calendar open, "oh...another five minutes. I'm so sorry to keep you waiting."

He was standing by the sofa and everything inside of him tightened and, at the same time, relaxed. Amilee! She was even more breathtaking than five years ago. Her fresh, lively beauty was almost a living force! Her energy vibrated through the room as he watched her bustle over to her desk, look at something, then nod as if her suspicions were confirmed.

"Let's get started," she announced, as she opened her purse. "So...let's get the worst of it over with first. How many prostitutes have you..." she paused, shuffling through her purse, "patronized this week?"

Prostitutes? What the hell? "None!" he stated firmly. He had never patronized a prostitute in his life! What the hell was she talking about? Why would she even ask someone that? Especially the man she was about to marry!

Okay, so perhaps she needed to know for health reasons. Prostitution carried a significant risk of sexually transmitted infections, so patronizing a prostitute could carry a risk of transmission to others. Namely her, since he was determined that they would be married. Soon!

Even as he thought it, his eyes moved to her round and enticing derriere as she bent over, rifling through a side drawer of her desk.

"Are you being perfectly honest with me?" she asked gently, moving to the other. "I can't help you through your addiction if you're not going to be honest with me."

Rian suddenly realized what she must be looking for and stepped closer.

Amilee felt the man come up behind her, startled that her client, who she'd been seeing for the past several months would approach her instead of staying in his favorite chair. But this wasn't the short, balding client she'd expected to see. This man was tall, with broad shoulders, and...goodness, he smelled absolutely delicious!

Suddenly, he reached towards her and she cringed slightly. But he only plucked something off her head and...with surprising gentleness, placed her glasses on her nose.

Suddenly, the world came into focus! And that focus sharpened when she realized that Rian, her betrothed, was smiling down at her.

"Rian!" she gasped. "What...what are you doing here?"

"Definitely not to discuss an addiction to prostitutes," he teased, those dark eyes gleaming down at her.

"Well,...um...."

"Could we have a seat? I think we have a great deal to discuss."

She glanced over at the sofa and chair, separated only by a coffee table and a box of tissues. "Yes!" she gasped, suddenly remembering that she needed to respond and not just stare blankly at her office furniture. "Of course." She bustled over to the chair where she normally sat, pushing her glasses higher onto her nose. "What are you doing here?"

He sat down across from her, but the sofa that had held so many others during her time helping clients through their traumas, seemed too small for Rian. He was too tall, too broad, and his knees bumped into the tiny coffee table.

"I would think that my presence here is obvious," he replied, crossing his legs and leaning back against the cushions. He stretched his arm along the back of the sofa as he watched Amilee's reaction. Her eyes shuttered and she frowned down at her notebook, one hand fluttering over her stomach. He knew her well enough now to recognize the gesture as a nervous habit.

"I don't know what you mean."

"During our last conversation, you asked for permission to obtain a graduate degree, and I granted that request."

Her jaw clenched and he wanted to laugh at her outrage. He was being pompous, but he wanted to rile her. Why? He had no idea. Perhaps so that he could see those charming dimples again. Or perhaps he wanted to reveal the woman behind the prim, boring clothes.

"I am still learning," she claimed. "In fact, just last weekend, I went to a conference about aberrant behavior in teenagers."

"Interesting, but irrelevant. I've read the letters you've sent over the past several years. And you are no longer enrolled at any university."

"Not true!" she gasped, sitting straighter in her chair. "I'm enrolled in a class at the University of Chicago and…"

"You are *teaching* that class, Amilee. Not attending the class as a student." His interjection of the facts seemed to deflate her and he didn't want that. "What's the problem?" he asked.

She bit her lip and looked out the window at the sky. But he doubted she saw anything outside the window. No, Amilee's thoughts were focused on something else.

"I don't *want* to marry you," she blurted out. She turned towards him and, for a moment, he was lost in the chocolate depths of those beautiful eyes. "I know that's a horrible thing to say, but I don't. I never wanted to become betrothed to you. And if you're honest with yourself, you couldn't have wanted this betrothal either. Not to mention the fact that it is an antiquated and ridiculous tradition. I was only twelve!"

"Your father signed as well."

Her eyes flared with fury. "I am not property!" she announced, clutching her notebook to her chest like a shield. "I'm an individual!"

"All very true," he agreed. "And yet, we are still betrothed according to the laws of Abidnae, of which you are a citizen."

Her chin lifted even as her eyes flashed with anger. "That can be changed."

He chuckled softly, shaking his head. "Because of your role, your position as my betrothed, I would need to sign off on any change in your citizenship."

Her eyes narrowed. "And would you grant that permission?"

He sighed, leaning forward. "Probably not."

With a hiss, she stood up and began pacing. "That's not fair!" she ground out between gritted teeth. "Why are you holding me to that stupid agreement?"

He stood up as well, moving towards her. He watched, almost amused as Amilee's eyes widened with surprise. That surprise morphed to nervousness as he moved closer still.

"Why am I not letting either of us out of the betrothal agreement?" he asked, his voice soft and gentle, not wanting to overwhelm her with the lust he felt. "Because several years ago, in a dark garden, this happened." And he kissed her.

For a long moment, she was stiff as he moved his lips over hers, nibbling and teasing. He pulled her closer until he could finally feel her glorious curves pressed against him. He knew the moment she gave in. Her lips softened and her hands moved to his shoulders. She angled her head and he deepened the kiss, feeling her press against him now. He tightened his arms, lifting her higher, their bodies fitting together perfectly as he nipped at her lower lip, silently commanding her to open for him. As soon as she did, his tongue moved in, tasting her.

Yes, this was the woman he remembered, Rian realized. This was the reaction that he wanted, needed, craved from her! When her fingers touched his neck, he felt his control slipping. With every ounce of control within him, he pulled back. As he looked down at her, Rian noticed that her lips were swollen, her eyes dreamy, and he could still feel her trembling with the same need he felt.

Unfortunately, the buzzer on her desk buzzed and he knew that he couldn't proceed with his plans. Not here. Especially since his plans included tossing her over his shoulder so that he could take her back to his penthouse and make love to her until she couldn't move.

Her eyes popped open at the sound and she looked around as if she didn't remember where she was. He liked that! A lot! At least he wasn't the only one struggling to retain control when they touched.

"I know you have clients," he told her, conceding that point at least. "So, we'll talk more about this over dinner." With that, he moved towards the door. "But Amilee, I've waited years for you. I'm not willing to keep waiting."

Amilee stared at the closed door, startled by his words. A less cynical person might assume that he actually desired her. That he was impatient to be with her.

But just as that hope began to bloom, another image overrode the first. Razeen. The memory returned and reality came thudding back to her. "Not again," she whispered furiously. Picking up her phone, she sent a text message.

"Emergency meeting! Need advice!"

Almost immediately, two messages chimed. "Lunch!" Annie, who worked on the ground floor of the building in the bakery, texted back. "I'll be there too!" Kate replied. Kate owned a boutique a few doors down from Annie, in the next building.

"Thanks! Park across the street?" It was their usual place to meet whenever they met for lunch during the warmer weather. Of course, those were few and far between in Chicago. The winters were brutally cold and windy while the summers could be stiflingly hot. Thankfully, it was a glorious spring day with temperatures in the mid-seventies. Amilee had needed a sweater on the drive into the office this morning, but by the time lunch came around, it would be warm enough for them to sit on a park bench. Of course, they'd need to get there early enough to get a park bench. On a beautiful, sunny day like today, everyone who worked in the downtown office buildings would emerge to enjoy a few minutes of sunshine.

Chapter 7

"Thanks for meeting me," Amilee said, hugging Kate and Annie.
They both sat down on a park bench, but Amilee resumed her pacing.
"What's going on?" Kate asked, peering into the brown bag and taking out one of the sandwiches that Amilee had bought at the deli down the street.
Amilee ran a hand over her stomach, clutching her own sandwich while Kate rummaged through the deli bag to find Annie's lunch.
Annie and Kate unwrapped their sandwiches while Amilee paced along the sidewalk in front of the bench. They munched and Amilee paced. Several times, Amilee lifted her forefinger into the air as if to say something, then stopped and continued pacing.
"She's going to explode," Annie whispered as she leaned towards Kate.
Kate nodded, wrinkling her nose as she popped another chip into her mouth. "It's going to be messy too!"
Amilee paused long enough to glare at her friends. "That's right. Laugh at the single chick. I know that you two are deliriously happy with your hubbies and," her eyes dropped to Annie's protruding belly, "are eagerly expecting your first child. But have a bit of sympathy for me. I just...!"
"If you'd date occasionally, maybe you'd find a keeper too," Annie interrupted.
That halted Amilee's pacing and she laughed weakly, letting her head fall back as she stared up into the trees. "Actually, I'm betrothed."
She lifted her head and stared at her two friends, enjoying their startled glances.
"Betrothed?" Annie echoed, lowering her sandwich until it rested on her swollen belly. "As in, *engaged*?"
Amilee shrugged and wobbled her head. "It's sort of the same thing."

Kate and Annie were staring wide-eyed at her, jaws nearly in their laps.

Amilee sighed, her chin dropping to her chest. "Actually, it's a bit more formal than an engagement."

"You're engaged," Kate whispered, then closed her eyes and shook her head, only to open her eyes again so that she could gawk at Amilee. "You're *betrothed*?!"

"To whom?" Annie interrupted. "When did this happen? Why didn't you tell us that you were seeing someone?" she demanded, sounding hurt.

"I haven't dated anyone," Amilee reassured both of them. "I was betrothed when I was twelve years old."

Kate choked. "That was seventeen years ago!"

Amilee laughed, but it wasn't an amused sound. "I know. I had to sign the damn betrothal contract in front of a couple hundred people! And in the frilliest, ugliest pink dress imaginable."

Annie leaned forward. "Who is it?"

Amilee bit her lip, clutching her still-wrapped sandwich closer to her chest. "The Sheik of Abidnae."

There was another, longer, silence. This time, it lasted so long, Amilee began to feel uncomfortable with their continued staring.

"That's sort of the reason why I never dated anyone. Why I turned down every guy you two tried to set me up with over the years."

"Because you were eng…uh…betrothed…to the freaking *Sheik of Abidnae*?" Kate whispered, then looked around as if to ensure that no one in the park could overhear. "Is it a secret betrothal?"

Amilee laughed. "No. It's not a secret." She sighed, pressing her forehead with her thumb and forefinger. "In fact, he's here, in town. Now. He came to my office this morning."

That statement caused another long silence as her friends stared up at her. Finally, Kate broke the silence when she ate another chip.

"What did he want?" Annie asked, balancing her sandwich on her stomach as she listened.

Amilee started pacing again, unable to keep still as she remembered what Rian had said this morning. "He says he's tired of waiting for me to come to him. He wants the wedding to take place immediately."

"Wow!" Kate whispered, snatching the sandwich off of Annie's stomach and taking a bite.

"Hey!" Annie yelped. "That's mine!"

"You weren't eating it and yours looks better than mine." She turned back to Amilee. "Isn't that sheik guy kinda hot?"

Amilee smiled crookedly. "Yeah. He's incredibly handsome. But…"

she bit her lip, then realized that she was squishing her sandwich and sighed, tossing it into the garbage before turning back to her friends. "The thing is...he kissed me. A long time ago." She hesitated, rolling her eyes. "Oh, and again, this morning."

Katy took another bite of Annie's sandwich, her eyes wide. Annie was much more verbal in her surprise. "He *kissed* you?"

"Yes."

Kate prompted, "And?" then crunched on another chip.

Amilee blinked. "And...what?"

Kate and Annie chuckled as they shared a knowing glance before turning back to her. "Was it enjoyable?"

Amilee's shoulders dropped. "Yes. Too enjoyable." She ran a hand over her forehead. "That's sort of the problem."

Kate leaned forward, shaking her head, causing her dark curls to dance around her shoulders. "Let me get this straight. You're engaged to a handsome man that you've been absolutely faithful to for...too long. He kissed you this morning and it was 'too enjoyable' but there's a problem?"

Amilee groaned, her hand fluttering over her hair. "The thing is, he doesn't know *me*. He doesn't have any real interest in me. He gives me gifts that are very pretty, but...but he is just as surprised by the gifts as I am when I open the box." She wiped away a stray tear. "And yes, when he kisses me, it's amazing and I lose myself in it, but..." she bowed her head. "After our first kiss several years ago, less than five minutes later, another woman, someone I absolutely loathe, was draped all over him."

"Did he kiss her right after kissing you?"

Amilee shook her head again. "No. Well, yes. But the way she was pressed against him, plus I noticed that his hands were on her hips and...oh, I left as quickly as I could. That was right before I started my third year of college." She resumed pacing, the words flowing now. "The agreement was that we'd be married as soon as I finished my education. At the time of the agreement, there was no expectation that I'd actually attend a college or university. The assumption was that I'd finish high school then attend a finishing school that would prepare me for my public life. After that, I'd be married and we'd start having babies and..." she shuddered, "and he'd go on living his life exactly as he wanted while I remained the dutiful, blind wife that ignores his mistresses and pretends that everything is wonderful and happy and... UH! I can't *stand* that woman!" she snapped, her hands fisting at her hips as she paced some more. "I hate her with every fiber in my body. And I hate him even more because I know, I can just tell by the familiar way they touch each other, that they were lovers!" Amilee made a rude sound as she pivoted and paced the other direction. "She makes my skin crawl. And the fact that he now wants me to drop everything, to go back to Abidnae and marry him, to pretend that my life is over simply so that I can produce babies for him and for the country so that there is an heir and a spare…it's just wrong! I'm not going to do it!"

There was a round of applause from Annie and Katy, who were delighted with their friend who, until this point, had been entirely non-emotional about men and dating.

Amilee blushed, chuckling at her friends. But she loved them.

"So, what are you going to do about it?" Kate asked, taking another bite of Annie's sandwich, ignoring Annie's glare.

"I don't know. I'm not sure how to get out of the betrothal. I don't want to put my father into a difficult situation. He's head of the intelligence agency in Abidnae. If I back out, then what will happen to his career?"

Kate waved a hand dismissively. "Let your father deal with that. He's the one who put you into this situation. Let him get himself out." Annie nodded her agreement and snatched the sandwich back before Kate managed to steal another bite.

"Yeah," Kate agreed around a mouthful of her own sandwich, pointing to Annie. "What she said."

Amilee chuckled. "I'm supposed to meet him for dinner tonight."

"Call and tell him that you're not going. That you're not interested in marriage to a man who will cheat on you and end the call."

Amilee smiled, relishing the thought of saying that to Rian. But a moment later, she shook her head, dismissing the idea. "I don't think it will be that easy."

Annie patted her tummy and fished an apple from the deli bag. "You won't know that until you tell him. And do it over the phone. You're stronger when you can't see someone's eyes."

"What do you mean?"

Kate chuckled. "You're a sucker for puppy-dog eyes, Amilee. And you know it."

"I am not!" she gasped.

"You are!" her friends replied in unison, then high-fived each other, grinning like the lunatics they were.

Kate continued, "Every time one of your clients has a problem, they give you that *look* and you melt into mush."

"I'm a good therapist!" she asserted, putting her hands on her hips.

Annie lifted a hand. "You're an amazing therapist…because you melt at their words. You care about them. Each and every one of them. You could have a serial killer in your office, sitting on that uncomfortable sofa that you love so much and..."

"My sofa is uncomfortable?" Amilee asked, eyes wide with surprise.

"It's like concrete," Kate answered, and took another bite as Annie continued.

"...and your clients spill their guts to you because they know that you truly care about them. What's more important, is that when you give them your sweet, caring look, they want to get better in order to help you feel better. And that's one of the reasons you're such a brilliant therapist. You care and the clients you help sense your concern and it soothes them deep down inside their soul where they need that healing. And they get better."

Kate nodded. "Yep. What she said."

"I'm quite eloquent today, aren't I?" Annie asked Kate.

Kate nodded her enthusiastic agreement. "Yes indeed!"

The two ladies turned to look at Amilee. "So?"

She stared at both of them. "That's your answer? I should just call him so that I can't see his eyes? I tell him I can't marry him and, because he's such a great guy, he'll just go about his business, head back to Abidnae, and find someone else to marry?"

Annie and Kate looked at each other. "It sounds like a good plan to me," Kate said with a shrug as she ate another chip.

Annie shrugged. "The alternative is to find some place to hide out for the rest of your life. I doubt that's what a good therapist would do, though."

Kate nodded. "Sort of the coward's way out."

Amilee bit her lip, her hand stroking her stomach before pushing her glasses higher up onto her nose. "I suppose it's the first step."

"Exactly," Kate agreed with a firm nod. She reached around Annie's big belly to grab the bakery box that Annie had brought. "What did you bring us for dessert?"

Amilee stared at her friend. Normally, Kate wasn't a big eater. But today, she'd not only eaten her sandwich, but half of Annie's, and was now perusing the bakery options? What was going on?!

"You're pregnant!" Amilee gasped, covering her own stomach with one hand and pointing at Kate's with the other. "Admit it, you totally are!"

Annie turned to gauge Kate's reaction, then gasped herself. "You are!"

Kate beamed and nodded as she selected the licorice filled donut with mint icing. "Yeah. Charles and I took the pregnancy test two days ago, but..." she shrugged. "We aren't going to tell anyone yet because it's too early. But I can't stop eating! I'm hungry all the time!"

Annie laughed, rubbing her swollen belly. "I know how it is. This little guy makes me hungry twenty-four seven! I eat like a horse and so far, I haven't gained any weight. My doctor is actually concerned about my lack of weight gain."

Amilee knelt down in front of her friend, touching Annie's knees. "Is everything okay with the baby though?"

"Yes," Annie said, still smiling. "He's fine. We had a sonogram last week and he's developing extremely well. I'm just hungry *all* the time. Just like Kate."

"Oh Annie!" Amilee said, leaning forward and kissing her belly. Kate leaned over as well and the three women started hugging, laughing, and crying all at the same time. It was a curious sight for the passersby, but the three friends didn't care. This was a special moment and Amilee felt a surge of protective love for her two friends who were both expecting their first child.

There was also a hint of jealousy. She wanted a family. Being an only child, she'd always longed for siblings. She'd begged her parents to give her a brother or sister, but her father was always so busy. And then... well, after her mother passed away, her father hadn't been interested in dating. His job and the pressure of his work made dating an issue.

As the three left the park, heading back to work, Amilee couldn't help but think that she might have had several children by now, if she hadn't witnessed Rian with Razeen so many years ago. She would have married him right after college, or maybe after grad school, and she'd be happy. Oblivious to his cheating ways.

Alas, she had seen that moment. And several others over the years. It wasn't until that one kiss that she'd thought about the other times that Razeen had touched or laughed with Rian. It was as if she knew something about Rian that no one else did.

Sighing, Amilee looked at her calendar for the rest of the afternoon. She had several more clients before she could head on home. But once there, she had a good bottle of wine from the cache her father had sent her last summer. She'd open one of those bottles and give Rian a call. Annie and Kate were right – it was time to set her expectations, which were none, since she expected nothing to happen between herself and Rian. She'd tell him that their betrothal was off and she'd wish him well as he looked for someone else to take her place.

He'd probably be relieved to be done with the betrothal. He most likely had several other women who were ready to take Amilee's place as the next queen of Abidnae.

With a heavy sensation in the region of her chest, a sensation that she couldn't seem to shake all afternoon, she worked with her clients, smiling when they told her of their successes over the past week, and nodding in understanding when they admitted their struggles. For each, she listened carefully, mindful of not falling for puppy dog gazes, and gave them additional exercises to work on over the next week.

Chapter 8

"I'll just be firm and precise, state my case, and that will be the end of it," Amilee declared, pulling the pins out of her hair as she kicked her black heels off. They landed somewhere in the corner of her den, not to be found again until the next time she needed them. Which was probably tomorrow, but she'd worry about that when she got there. Tonight, she had other things to worry about. Such as unbetrothing herself to a man she didn't really want to marry!

She'd called Rian from her office, but he hadn't been available to speak with her. The aide she'd spoken with had warned Amilee that Rian would come to her apartment tonight. No matter how much Amilee argued, the results remained the same; Rian was on his way here.

Rushing into her bedroom, she pulled off the black suit she'd worn to work and grabbed an old pair of leggings and a man's shirt she'd picked up at a thrift store. As she pulled her hair up into a ponytail, she checked her reflection in the mirror over her dresser. "If this doesn't send the right signal, nothing will."

As soon as she stepped out of her bedroom, a pair of soft, fluffy socks covering her feet, the doorbell rang. She pulled the door open, knowing she would find Rian on the other side. Sure enough, he was there, looking handsome, tall, and extremely forbidding. His eyes narrowed as they traveled down over her figure before coming back up to her face. "Am I to understand that we are dining in tonight?" he asked.

Amilee gripped the doorknob tightly, nodding as she opened the door further to allow him to come inside. "Do your guards need to come in as well?"

He glanced back at them and, with a nod, Rian walked inside. Two guards took up sentry duty outside her door while the other two went back downstairs to...wherever it was that they would be until Rian left for the evening.

"Your assistant told me that you were on your way, even though we could have discussed this on the phone." She took a deep breath, letting it out slowly to calm her nerves. "I thought it would be easier to talk here rather than in a restaurant. You draw a great deal of attention when you go out in public."

"You make a good point," he agreed as she closed the door. When she turned around, she watched in fascination as he loosened the knot of his tie, tossing it over a chair. He unbuttoned the top three buttons of his dress shirt, and slid out of his jacket, tossing it over his tie.

"You...what are you doing?" she demanded, backing up a step. Immediately, her reaction to his kiss came to mind.

"I'm getting more comfortable," he explained, looking around. "Ah, you've opened a bottle of wine. Excellent!"

"Yes. Would you like a glass?" she asked, rushing into the kitchen to pull two glasses down out of a cabinet, relieved to have something to do with her hands.

"Yes, that would be nice. Thank you." He lifted the bottle, examining the label. "This is a good vintage. Did your father send it to you?"

Amilee took umbrage at his assumption. "Why? You don't think that I can afford a bottle of wine?"

He laughed softly. "Don't get angry, my dear," he said, taking a glass and filling it. "I had dinner with your father two weeks ago and he served this wine. He mentioned that it was his favorite."

"Oh," she replied, feeling silly for becoming defensive. "I'm sorry about that."

"But I also know that you wouldn't be able to afford this bottle of wine as well as pay your rent. They are about the same and I know how much you earn as a salary."

Her eyes lifted, angry once again. "How? How do you know those details?"

He moved closer, handing her the glass. "Because I took an interest in what you do and the details of your life several years ago, my dear."

"An interest in my life does not mean that you have the right to..." she stopped her tirade when he touched her cheek with his hand.

"You are a little porcupine, aren't you?" he teased. "My interest was not merely for my own benefit, Amilee," he explained softly. "It was also to ensure your safety. As my betrothed, you are in danger from my enemies. My security team was tasked with ensuring that you were protected, although I demanded that they do so from a distance so that you could enjoy life as a college student for as long as possible."

"Well, I guess that's...um...okay."

"You think so?" he laughed, moving even closer. "Why did you want to speak with me here, in private, my porcupine?"

Amilee might have laughed at his teasing, but his hand lingered on her cheek and she was startled by the intensity of emotions that a simple touch could invoke. "I just...I wanted to–"

Her explanation was forgotten as he lowered his head to kiss her. Just like this morning, his touch was soft at first. When she didn't pull away, he lifted his lips, looking down at her. "You have the softest lips," he murmured, and kissed her again.

"They aren't soft," she argued.

He grinned slightly. "And the porcupine emerges with all points ready to stab."

"I'm not a porcupine," she whispered, pulling away. But her voice wasn't nearly as strong as she'd like it to be. It was soft and wavering, showing how affected she was by his touch.

Stepping around him, she walked into the family room, keeping her back to him. "We need to talk, Rian."

"I'm here. What shall we discuss?"

She swung around, relieved that he'd paused in her kitchen doorway, leaning against the doorjamb.

"I don't want to be betrothed to you anymore," she blurted. Her eyes widened as she realized how blunt that came out. But she didn't back down. She waited, holding her breath to see how he would react.

"I agree," he replied, pushing away from the wall and coming towards her.

"You do?" she squeaked, her breath rushing out of her lungs in a whoosh! "Oh, that's such a relief! I thought you'd be angry!"

He laughed softly. "Why would I be angry? It's the main reason I came here to talk with you."

"It is?" she asked, laughing again, almost dizzy with relief. There was a strange pang of...something she wasn't willing to define. "Well, good! I mean, we should...figure out what to say to...I don't even know who would care."

He lifted a brow. "The world will care, my dear. The whole world is waiting for an announcement."

"Seriously?" She watched as he sat down at the far end of the sofa. "Why?"

He gestured for her to sit and, even though she didn't feel like sitting down, she did so, although at the other end of the sofa.

"Why wouldn't everyone be waiting to hear about our wedding? It's been planned for too long and our people are ready for news of the event."

Amilee jumped back to her feet, taking a step away from him. "Wait. What?"

That eyebrow lifted again. "The wedding? Isn't that what this is all about?"

She shook her head. "No!" she replied, waving her hands. "Definitely not! This is about *ending* our betrothal!"

"Exactly," he said, crossing his legs so that his ankle rested on his knee. It was such an American gesture that it caught her off guard.

"No, we're not ending the betrothal with a wedding. We're just…ending the betrothal!" she told him firmly.

He laughed and stood up. "Why would we do that?"

She sputtered for a long moment before she finally blurted out, "Because we don't want to get married to each other?"

He shook his head. "But I would be delighted to marry you."

She stared at him as if he'd lost his mind. "No you wouldn't!"

He reached for her hands but she stepped out of range.

"Amilee, why would I not want to be married to you? You're beautiful, intelligent, sensitive, and…"

"And I don't want to get married!" she snapped. "Not to you or…actually, not to anyone. But especially not to you!"

Those annoying eyebrows lifted again. "Why 'especially' not to me?"

Amilee wasn't sure what to say to that. "Your Highness, our betrothal was…it was agreed upon years ago. We were too young. We shouldn't have agreed to something that significant. You were barely twenty years old and I was twelve! That's not how solid relationships are formed!"

"That's true. And if we hadn't gotten to know one another over the years, if I hadn't discovered what a truly intelligent and fascinating person you were, then I would agree that the betrothal should be put aside. But that's not the case. Is it? We *are* attracted to each other."

"No! I'm not!"

"I believe that I disproved that statement earlier today," he argued softly. "Should I prove it again?" he asked, stepping closer.

Rian watched with a mixture of fascination and fury as Amilee argued to put aside the betrothal. He'd been fascinated with Amilee since she was a mere fourteen years old. He'd become sexually attracted to her when she'd stepped into the palace at twenty, her femininity only beginning to blossom. He'd been furious with himself during that visit, holding himself back from kissing her when she was too young, even thinking himself a deviant for thinking such lustful thoughts about a girl so young. Then at twenty, that kiss, the way she'd looked and the beauty of her lush curves...she'd driven him wild that night! It had taken all of his control to step away from her!

And yet, he'd waited. The terms of the betrothal contract were that they would wed after she'd finished her education. Now was the time. He'd waited long enough!

"No!" she stopped him by waving a hand. "There's no need to prove anything, Your Highness."

If she'd said his name, he might have cooled a bit of his temper. But hearing her use his title only inflamed him further. "Amilee, are you trying to provoke me?" he demanded.

"No!" she gasped. "Why would you even suggest something like that?"

"Because you refuse to use my given name after I have repeatedly given you permission to use it."

She laughed, shaking her head. "Do you have any idea how arrogant you sound? You've 'given me permission to use your first name', and yet you use my first name all the time. When did I ever give *you* permission to use my name? I don't recall ever giving you that honor."

"You know perfectly well that there are different standards, etiquette that we must adhere to. I don't like some of the stupider rules either. And I absolutely hate that you won't use my name."

"Why would I?" she demanded, folding her arms over her stomach. That only pushed her breasts up higher, utterly distracting him.

He growled and stepped closer, his temper barely leashed. He would prove to her that they had a connection, one that they both needed to recognize and embrace. No woman had ever affected him the way she did!

"So, if I were to touch you like this," he purred, trailing a hand down her arm. "You wouldn't like it, would you?"

Amilee opened her mouth to speak, but the words stuck in her throat. She stared up at him, afraid to move for fear she'd start shaking. He reached out and ran a hand lightly down her other arm. "Or like this?" he asked, his voice deepening as he watched her nipples harden, proving that he affected her. If she were to simply look down, she'd see that he was aching for her.

"Or would you like me to kiss you?" he asked. "Would that prove that we're attracted to each other?"

"It wouldn't prove anything," she muttered, but her eyes dropped to his mouth.

"Are you sure?" he asked, his voice husky, his lips barely a centimeter from hers, his breath warm against her face.

She opened her mouth to deny him, but he kissed her. The electric sizzle that jolted through her startled her and she grabbed onto his shirt. This wasn't like the slow, simmering kiss from this morning. Nope, this was hot and sultry, his mouth forcefully demanding entry and, when he nipped at her lips, she gasped, opening to his invasion. And oh, what a sweet invasion it was! She whimpered, pulling him closer, needing to press herself against his hardness. A part of her wondered why she was doing this, but the other part told that first part to shut up and enjoy herself.

Then there was no thinking at all. It was all just muddled thoughts that sounded something like, "Don't stop" and "Do that again." For all she knew, Amilee could be saying them out loud.

She felt a burning sensation on her back, then realized that it was his hands touching her bare skin. She wanted more, wanted to feel his skin against her own. Just a brief touch, she promised herself as she unbuttoned his shirt. A few of the buttons didn't give fast enough and there might have been a ping somewhere in her apartment when a button flew through the air. Amilee didn't care! This...this she remembered from her dreams before that first kiss. Except this...was so much better! She never could have imagined feeling this hot and bothered and wildly needy! Her imagination simply wasn't that good!

He lifted her up and pinned her to the wall. She felt something press against her core and she definitely cared about that. It pressed and she rolled her hips entreatingly, sending more of those delicious electric shocks throughout her body. But it wasn't enough! Not nearly enough! She needed to feel more of him, her hands exploring his skin. She heard him groan, and interpreted that as permission to continue. When he ripped his shirt off, she sighed with relief as she ran her hands over his chest. Then his hands were touching her. She had no idea where her shirt went...and her leggings were down to her knees.

He shifted against her and all thoughts of her leggings disappeared from her mind as she pressed against him, wanting, needing more. She shivered, gasping for air, but nothing seemed to satisfy her until she rolled her hips again! Higher and tighter, her body seemed to spiral upwards until...stars burst in front of her eyes as pleasure pulsed through her, around her, inside of her, and she screamed.

And then nothing! She slumped forward, her arms clutching at Rian as he lifted her carefully into his arms. She might have laughed. Or was it a sob? All she knew was that she was cradled in his arms and she knew that she wanted to be here forever!

"That was beautiful, Amilee," he groaned as he laid her down on her bed.

Amilee smiled up at him, more relaxed than she'd ever felt before.

"That was amazing!" she sighed.

"Think you can do it again?"

He pulled her leggings completely off, tossing them away.

She laughed again, feeling...odd. "No. Probably not."

He kissed the inside of her leg. Gone were those nice, wonderful sensations. The floating feeling was gone, replaced by an intense need.

"Let's try anyway, shall we?"

His mouth covered her breast and Amilee gasped, her body tightening all over again. "Rian!"

"That sounds amazing. Say it again!" he ordered.

She shook her head, but his mouth closed over her nipple. She might have said his name, or it could have been a scream. Regardless, she arched her back, offering herself up to him. Needing that strange, vibrating tension. She recognized it this time and, stunned, wanted to experience it again.

"Rian, I don't know what's happening," she whispered to him, frantic as she rubbed her legs along his hips. He was still clothed and she didn't like that. She needed...she wasn't sure. It was too much and she tried to pull his head away.

"Stay there," he ordered, standing up as he stripped off his clothes.

Amilee wanted to tell him to stop, but he was so beautiful. With every piece of clothing that he discarded, she admired what he revealed. The muscles along his arms and chest rippled with power. Then his hands moved to his slacks, unbuttoning them, sliding the zipper down. Slowly. Was he stripping for her benefit? Amilee couldn't look up at his face to determine his point. She watched, her mouth dry as he slid the material down his legs. He stepped out of his slacks and his boxers, tossing them to the side. Then he stood there beside the bed, completely naked, allowing her time to take him in.

"You can touch me, you know," he said, his voice rough with passion. She gazed up at him, then back down at that magnificent erection.

"How?" she asked, her mouth dry and her eyes wide with fascination.

He took her hand. "Like this," he said, then wrapped her fingers around his shaft, moving her hand slowly up and down. She took over, exploring, feeling the velvety softness covering the steel underneath.

"Let me see all of you, Amilee," he ordered, taking her knees and spreading them wide.

For a moment, she was horrified that he would look at her in such an intimate way, but then he lowered his head, his mouth nuzzling those dark curls and...

"Oh dear heaven!" she gasped, her hands sliding into his hair as her hips twitched at the unexpected sensation. "Don't..."

"You don't like it?"

Her muffled response was almost laughable, but he understood and bent his head, his mouth teasing and torturing her as her body tightened with desire and need.

"Not this time, love," he said, chuckling as he kissed his way back up her body. He spent a few extra moments teasing her nipples again, but then he was there, kissing her so she could taste herself on his lips as he wrapped her legs around him, shifting her hips so that she cradled him more intimately.

Amilee felt his throbbing erection pressing against her opening, but all she could do was tense up, her body ready for this, needing him to fill her. She didn't fully understand this driving need, although she knew the mechanics of the sexual act. Of course she knew! No one in this day and age was unaware of sex. The confusing part was this desperate need, this all encompassing desire for him to fill her, to connect with her in the most intimate of ways, that she didn't recognize or understand.

As he pressed into her, she felt a small pinch of pain, but once he was fully inside of her, he stilled.

"Are you okay?"

She thought about it for a long moment, her fingers curling around his upper arms. "Yes?"

He laughed, his arms starting to shake with the effort to control himself. "I hurt you."

Oh! Is that what he was worried about? "I'm fine," she told him, shifting her hips. "It's nothing at all."

He bent down, kissing her tenderly as he started to thrust himself into her. With a gasp, Amilee moved with him. The friction was…no, it wasn't nice. It was…odd. Her body felt so tight and tense that she didn't know what to do.

"Rian, should I…?"

"Just enjoy, Amilee," he whispered into her ear, smiling as she trembled. "Relax, and move in whatever way makes you feel good."

So, she did. And whoa! "I don't…its too much, Rian," she muttered, gripping his hips to try to still him.

He only laughed, a husky sound that made her body tighten even further as he grabbed her hands and pinned them over her head. He clasped her wrists in one hand while the other moved down over her body, his thumb teasing that sensitive nub and…!

"Rian!" she screamed as her body exploded, the throbbing pleasure overwhelming her. She clung to him as he released her hands, pounding faster and faster into her heat until he groaned, collapsing on top of her.

After a moment, he rolled to his side, bringing her with him so that she was draped over his chest. Amilee couldn't move, too shocked by what had just occurred.

Chapter 9

Amilee woke the following morning before her alarm. Or was it after? The sun was shining but she had no idea what time it was. One thing she was positive about though; her body was sore in places she hadn't known even existed. Stretching her legs, muscle by muscle, just to make sure everything was in working order, she slowly sat up so that she was sitting on the edge of her bed. And yes, she was almost painfully tender "down there". Finding her glasses, she slipped them on and looked around, trying to figure out what, and why, last night had happened.

Glancing at her phone, which she hadn't remembered putting on the bedside table last night, she noticed that it was, thankfully, still relatively early. She had plenty of time to take a long, hot shower.

Groaning, she got slowly out of bed and made her way to the shower. Shoving her glasses higher up on her nose, Amilee noticed her room was a mess and she had no idea how the pillows had ended up in her closet. She also noticed that her clothes had been picked up and draped over the chair in the corner of her room. Rian's clothes were gone and Amilee vaguely remembered Rian waking her up earlier this morning, or last night? To kiss her goodbye. He'd said something about meeting with her tonight, but that was all she could remember. Maybe more of it would come back after a shower and coffee. Lots of coffee!

"No more sex!" she whispered as she stepped under the hot spray. Gently, she soaped herself, feeling every ache and stretch of overworked muscles. As her fingers rubbed the soap against her body, she shivered, remembering how Rian had touched her in the same places, how his mouth had tasted her and he'd encouraged her to taste him and...!

"Stop it!" she ordered to the bathroom. Rinsing off, she stepped out of the shower to dry off, but the normally soft towel was too rough on certain areas of her body. Looking down at her thighs, she realized that there were several red patches. "What in the world?!"

That's when Amilee remembered what Rian had been doing down there and…and what must have happened! His jaw, his mouth, and… and the tender skin of her inner thighs!

"I'm going to kill him!" she muttered, selecting a pair of slacks for work today, needing a bit of protection from her thighs from chaffing. "I need coffee!"

An hour later, she walked into her office, smiling to Rebecca, the receptionist, who gave her an odd look. Amilee self-consciously smoothed down her hair and nudged her glasses higher up on her nose with her finger, wondering if last night's sexual marathon showed. Her lips were a bit swollen, but that was about it. She didn't have any red patches on her face, although that was a miracle, considering how much they'd kissed last night. How could the skin of her thighs be so badly abraded while her face was fine?

"Good morning, Rebecca," she called out, forcing a smile since her lips were chapped. Another lovely memento from last night, she thought as she grabbed the client files for her morning sessions and made her way down the long hallway towards her office.

As soon as she turned the corner though, she saw the guards. "Oh no," she muttered, pausing but her approach caught the attention of both guards who turned, watching her with their usual bland expressions. A blush stole up her cheeks as she realized that these men, or some other men on their team, had stayed up all night guarding Rian while he was inside her apartment doing…things…to her! Even worse, every guard on Rian's team knew that he had spent the night in her apartment. In her bed! They all knew…everything! Well, not everything. But they would figure it out!

With her head held high, she forced her feet down the hallway. But instead of stepping into her office, where she knew Rian awaited her, she bowed her head, took a deep breath, then looked at the guards. "I apologize for keeping His Highness out so late last night. It won't happen again."

The men, obviously unused to someone apologizing to them, stared at her for a long moment, turned to look at each other as if silently saying, "Huh?!" then looked back down at her without responding.

Her office door opened and Rian stood there, tall, dark, and intimidating in a charcoal suit and red tie.

"You're late," he announced, taking her hand and pulling her into her office.

"I am?" she asked, glancing at the clock on the wall. "I'm not late," she argued. "I'm actually an hour early. I always get in early to review my client files before their appointments."

That's when the scent of bacon hit her and she looked around. "What's all this?"

"Breakfast," he told her, handing her a cup of coffee as he led her to the sofa. "You need a different sofa. This one is miserable."

"So I've heard," she mumbled, sitting down on it and… "Wow, this is really awful!" she agreed, trying to find a soft spot on the stupid couch. But it was a solid sofa and there wasn't any place where it wasn't stiff.

"You need breakfast," he announced, uncovering and handing her a plate. "You didn't have dinner last night so I know that you're hungry."

She didn't mention that she'd skipped lunch yesterday as well, mostly because he'd ask her why and Amilee wasn't willing to admit visiting her friends and the topic of their conversation. That would be too… well, the word "private" popped into her mind, but considering everything that they'd done last night, she wasn't sure that anything could be more private than that.

So instead, she lifted her fork and forced herself to smile. "Thank you. This is lovely."

He picked up the other plate and started eating. "I'm sorry that I wasn't with you this morning when you woke up. Are you okay?"

Amilee's fork froze midway to her mouth. "Um…" she could feel her cheeks burning. "I'm fine," she finally managed. "Everything is fine. I'm fine."

He laughed softly. "You are sore, aren't you?"

That silly blush intensified. "I'm fine. Nothing that a hot shower couldn't fix."

A dark eyebrow lifted challengingly and Amilee guessed that he wanted more information. "And your thighs?"

She'd just looked down at her plate but his words had her head snapping right back up. "My thighs? What's wrong with my thighs?"

He smiled slightly, his eyes heating up as he looked at her lap. "I shaved before I came to pick you up, but I'm guessing that, as the night wore on and our…activities…didn't abate, that the skin on your inner thighs might be–"

"I'm fine!" she yelped, horrified that he was thinking about her thighs, inner or otherwise. "My skin is perfectly fine!"

He laughed softly, his gaze moving to her neck. "I see that, in my zealousness last night, I left a mark."

Amilee's fork clattered to the plate and her hand flew to her neck. "Oh god!" she gasped, eyes wide as she remembered Rebecca's expression earlier. "Where?"

He touched her neck, his finger sliding against the base right where her pulse throbbed. "Right here. You're very sensitive along your neck and collarbone. I'm sorry for marking you, but in my defense, every time I touched you there, you moaned and wiggled. It was rather intoxicating."

"Oh no!" she groaned, closing her eyes as she tried to shift her blouse to cover the spot. "I think I have some makeup in my purse." Standing up, she realized that her legs were more than a little shaky. Grabbing her purse, she tried to ignore the throbbing need building up inside of her, and the desire to curl up on his lap and beg him to do those naughty, delicious things to her all over again.

"You're so beautiful when you're embarrassed, Amilee," he told her with a chuckle, leaning back against the hard cushions of the sofa as he took a bite of the eggs, sausage, and crispy fried potatoes that he'd brought them for breakfast.

"I'm not sure that's something I'm striving for, Your Highness," she grumbled, pulling a compact out and dabbing a bit of powder over the offending bruise. It didn't help much and she groaned, snapping the compact closed. "I have a scarf around here somewhere." She walked around her desk, rummaging through the drawers.

"I'll have my assistant procure a scarf for you," he offered, typing away on his phone. "It will be here before your first appointment."

He stood up and walked over to her, stopping her with just a touch. "It is not my intention for our intimate time together to become public knowledge. Our lovemaking will be private."

She was too stunned by his touch to respond immediately, but as soon as she stepped back, Amilee shook her head. "We won't have any more intimate times together," she told him firmly. "And last night wasn't making love, it was just sex, Your Highness. Good sex but–"

He snorted and moved closer, wrapping his arm around her waist, pulling her against him. "You don't have enough experience to properly judge, so I will excuse your incorrect description of last night as merely 'good'. In reality, it was amazing. And don't even try to deny that you feel the same way about it. I felt your body tremble with every release last night. I tasted your climax on my tongue and knew the intimate joy of having your body clench around my shaft as you screamed your pleasure."

"Stop it!" she whispered fervently, worried her cheeks would actually catch fire. "It wasn't–"

His eyes darkened with her denial. "Don't you dare try and belittle what occurred between us last night, Amilee. It was wonderful and it *will* happen again. Many times, in fact. I am looking forward to married life so that we can properly enjoy the physical intimacies of our relationship."

"I don't...!"

Whatever she'd been about to say was forgotten as he kissed her senseless. By the time he straightened, she was clinging to him, practically unable to stand.

"Your...."

He kissed her again and Amilee sighed with longing, unable to deny him when he kissed her.

When he straightened again, she glared up at him, pushing out of his arms. "Are you going to kiss me every time I do or say something you don't agree with?"

"Yes. It's very effective," he admitted, moving back to the sofa and picking up his plate. "Please, let's eat breakfast and you can tell me about your day. I know that you're hungry."

Amilee was, but not necessarily for food. But because she wasn't willing to admit it, she picked up her plate, although she sat on the chair instead of the couch. The small coffee table wasn't much of a defense, but it was better than nothing, she rationalized.

"This is wonderful," she said, needing to break the silence between them. She nibbled on the eggs, and realized how hungry she truly was. "Oh, this is absolutely fantastic!"

"What kinds of patients will you see today?"

Amilee shook her head. "I can't discuss my patients, Your..." she stopped when he shot her a warning look. She wouldn't say his name, but she continued with what she'd been about to say. "Since I can't talk about my patients, why don't you tell me what you're doing today? What kinds of meetings are you attending?"

"I'm meeting with several business leaders who are interested in investing in Abidnae, but I'm not sure if they are the right kind of people to move into the country. I don't want them taking advantage of our people, so I might put some obstacles in their way in an effort to convince them to choose another country."

"How could they abuse our people?" she asked, stabbing a big, crispy potato chunk.

"Two of them want to build resorts on an ocean front property. Those jobs are low paying and the businesses rape the environment. Most of them don't promote the employees who come from the local population, even if they have the experience and education for the higher paying jobs. And they put too many chemicals into the environment to make their invasive landscaping thrive. That's not the type of investments that we want."

"So, how will you stop them?"

He shrugged. "I could simply deny them access to the land. But the best way is to make the property taxes too high and require a living wage for the workers. The problem is that some areas of Abidnae are so desperate for work that they'd take even the low paying jobs. Until they get used to that level of lifestyle. Then they'll want more, but there won't be 'more' after some types of industries take over a region. The resort executives and non-citizens have curtailed the local officials from enforcing the local laws. It's a vicious cycle I'd like to avoid."

"That's horrible!" she gasped. "I didn't know that the resorts were such a bad investment."

"Some aren't. I don't know enough about these particular companies to make that determination. That's why I'm sitting down with them to listen to their proposals."

"That's very good of you," she said with a smile, genuine admiration showing in her eyes.

Rian watched Amilee, wondering if she knew how beautiful she was. She was always lovely, her dark eyes and lush, raven hair ensured that. But today, she appeared more relaxed.

Perhaps it was simply that he knew her body now. He knew what she felt like in his arms, pressed against his body. He knew what she felt like when she shivered with a climax. He knew that she opened her mouth during every beautiful release. Last night had been a heady experience. Even knowing that she'd been a virgin until last night made his body ache with the need to be with her again.

He finished off his breakfast, relieved to see that she'd eaten more than half of hers as well. "How many clients do you have today?" he asked, wiping his hands with a napkin.

She glanced over at the stack of files on her desk. "I think I have four this morning and five this afternoon. Only one tonight though, which is good."

"What time do you finish?"

She eyed him warily and he wanted to laugh. Did she really think that could discourage him? Not a chance! Even before he knew what a sensuous beauty she was, he'd wanted her. Now that he knew of her delights, he was even more enamored. He wanted the wedding accomplished immediately. Even now, he was planning a long honeymoon. Two weeks of nothing but teaching Amilee the joys of lovemaking. Mentally, he made a list of all of the positions he was going to teach her once they were alone. Tonight, for instance…he could…!

She stood up, shoving her glasses higher up on her nose in that nervous habit of hers before taking their plates over to the wicker basket that his housekeeper had packed for their breakfast. "I really need to get to work. I like to review my client notes before they come in. So I'm sorry, but you have to go."

She turned, her hands folded primly in front of her and he swallowed a laugh. Instead, he pulled her into his arms. "Until tonight," he promised, kissing her until he felt her melt in his arms. Damn, he loved kissing the stiffness out of her!

Pulling back, he almost groaned at the tightness in his body. "Do you want to go out for dinner? Or should I pick you up and take you back…?"

"Out," she interrupted. He almost laughed, knowing that her preference for being in a public restaurant was merely to stop him from kissing her. Little did she know, a public place couldn't stop the inevitable.

"I'll pick you up after work then," he said, kissing her forehead as he left the office. At the doorway, he pointed to the basket. "Someone will come by to collect that." And he walked out, clenching his fists to stop himself from reaching for her again.

Amilee eyed the basket, wondering how a man as arrogant and domineering as Rian could also be so sweet and sensitive. The dichotomy was…confusing, to say the least.

Fortunately, Amilee didn't have time to waste. She had clients who needed her help and she wasn't going to sit around trying to figure that man out. She had much better things to do!

Over the next several hours, she listened to her clients and talked them through their issues. Each one was struggling with addiction, grief, or problems in their life that they couldn't handle on their own. Amilee guided them through their issues, feeling their pain as well as their hope as they walked out the door.

By lunchtime, she was a bit behind in her schedule, so she'd decided to skip lunch to review her afternoon client files and get caught up. She hated having her clients wait for her. They already felt invisible or helpless. She didn't want to add to the sense of being a burden.

She closed her office door and pulled the stack of files for her afternoon clients, intending to review her notes so that she was fully prepared for her afternoon sessions.

Unfortunately, her plan was not to be. A knock on the door warned her that her efforts would be dismantled. If it was Rian, she was going to tell him to go away. She answered the door warily. If it were one of her co-workers, she'd tell them to leave her alone. Nicely, she reminded herself as fatigue slowed her steps. Last night had been relaxing in some ways, but it hadn't been very good for her sleep cycles.

But when she opened the door, it wasn't Rian's formidable frame standing in the hallway. It was actually the last person she would have expected.

"Inis!" she gasped, stepping forward to embrace the frail, elderly woman. "Goodness, it's wonderful to see you!"

The woman smiled when Amilee pulled back, her dark eyes twinkling with humor and affection. "Am I interrupting your lunch break?" she asked.

Amilee quickly shook her head. "Not at all. Please come in!" she lied. "What brings you all the way out here? I thought you rarely left the palace in Abidnae."

"That's true," she said with wry humor. "But my grandson called me last night to tell me that he was getting married soon. I flew out here right after that call to find out if it was true." She sat down heavily on the sofa, cringing. "Goodness, this sofa is awful."

Amilee laughed and sat down on the other end of the piece of miserable furniture. "I know. I bought it on impulse because I liked the retro look of it. But I didn't realize it was so uncomfortable until just recently."

"Ghastly thing!" Inis muttered, shifting her elderly frame on the cushions. "But I didn't come here to discuss décor. I came because I was worried about you, dear." She looked at Amilee with a steady gaze. "What's this I hear about you and my grandson getting married?"

Amilee waved a hand dismissively. "Oh, that's just his wishful thinking. I'm definitely not…" she paused, remembering who she was talking to. "I mean, it isn't the fact that your grandson isn't a very nice man. It's just that–"

"Oh pish, my dear. We've never had the kind of relationship where we beat around the bush about these things. I know exactly how you feel, Amilee. I also know why you avoided coming to the palace to celebrate either your birthday or Rian's the past few years. And don't think I haven't noticed that you still refuse to use his first name." She settled herself more comfortably. "So, what's going on? Why are you marrying my grandson when things still aren't settled between you two?"

Amilee laughed. "You were always too observant for my peace of mind, Inis," she replied. "I haven't agreed to shift the betrothal to a wedding. Your grandson has a mind of his own and has simply decreed that we will marry at once."

"I remember the betrothal contract stating that you wouldn't marry until your education was finished. And, I know that you are still attending classes on the weekends at the University of Chicago. Are you close to completing your doctoral degree?"

She smiled, nodding. "Yes. I'm very close." Amilee didn't add that she might be teaching those classes, although it was entirely possible that Inis already knew that.

"So, why would you stop now just to get married?" Inis demanded. "Don't you know that the women in our country need a role model like you? They need someone to show these men that women can be strong and powerful, and also feminine and lovely!"

Amilee laughed. "No pressure, right?"

Inis waved her comment away. "None at all! So why? Why are you marrying him? And don't even try to tell me that you're in love with him. I simply won't believe it!"

Amilee sighed, looking down at her hands folded politely on her lap. "To be honest, I'm not sure if I even like your grandson."

Inis sat back, nodding with a satisfactory smile on her elderly features. "Excellent response!"

Amilee's eyes widened, surprised at the older woman's words. "Don't you *want* me to marry your grandson?" Amilee asked, slightly hurt.

"Of course I do," she replied quickly. "But Rian has had everything so easy in his life. He definitely needs a challenge. And you, my dear, are the perfect challenge for him. You're bright and intelligent, savvy and ambitious. Plus, I also know that Rian is absolutely wild about you."

"He is not," Amilee argued.

"Of course he is," she countered. "But you're not going to believe that. You're not ready to believe it. Besides," she continued with a mischievous twinkle in her eyes, "you need my grandson to prove it to you. So don't you give up, my dear!"

Amilee sighed, wishing that life was as simple as Inis believed it to be. "I'm not sure if I can hold him off. He seems pretty determined to get the wedding over with and on to…well, whatever it is that he wants to move on to."

Inis' eyes sparkled as she took in Amilee's appearance. "If I know my grandson, and I do," she emphasized, "then I'm pretty sure that the 'thing' he wants to move on to is the honeymoon. But you, Amilee, need to show him what he almost gave up."

Amilee wasn't sure what she meant. Was she losing her mind? "I've never been something he could give up. We've been betrothed for a long time." She shrugged as if that fact didn't bother her. "I'm sort of a sure thing."

"Not at all!" Inis took Amilee's hand with her gnarled fingers. "Dear, you kissed him that night, didn't you? On your twentieth birthday?"

Amilee didn't want to remember that night. She started to shake her head, only to have Inis smile reassuringly.

"I know you did. I'm guessing it was a sweet kiss. Maybe even your *first* kiss?" she asked, hopefully.

Amilee looked away, not wanting to remember the pain of that night. "Well..."

"Aha!" Inis clapped her arthritic hands together. "That's delightful!" she laughed, reaching out to squeeze Amilee's fingers. "And after that wonderful kiss, you saw that horrid creature. I've always hated that girl. Razeen." Inis almost spat after saying the other woman's name. "She's toxic!"

Amilee's lips pressed together for a long moment before she continued. "She's lovely. And would probably be a better wife for Rian than I could be."

Inis made a rude sound and Amilee couldn't stifle her laughter.

"Don't you dare give in! I know how you feel for Rian. I also suspect that his feelings for you are significantly deeper than he realizes! And that Razeen!" Inis pretended to spit off to the side. "She's a pox that will only make him miserable!" Inis added a nod for emphasis. Then her features softened. "No, my dear. You are the woman my grandson needs. He needs your understanding and your sweetness. But he also needs your stubbornness and your determination." She beamed and the beauty of her expression stunned Amilee. "You are good for my grandson," she said, nodding in emphasis. "And what's more, I think that my grandson is good for you." Her eyes dropped to Amilee's neck where a soft, pink scarf covered up the dark spot left from last night's activities, a slow, triumphant smile forming on her wrinkled face.

"I think you're a crafty old woman, Inis," Amilee laughed, delighted with her attitude as well as her pronouncement. "But I'm not going to marry your grandson."

Inis chuckled. "I get it. But how about this," she suggested. "There is a hospital opening this weekend. There are many events planned to celebrate this event, including a discussion panel in the morning on mental health issues. I've already added your name as one of the panelists and this would give you a significant amount of exposure." She tilted her head slightly. "Will you come? Talk on the panel, give us your ideas, and..." her eyes twinkled, "...show my grandson what a fool he was to kiss another woman only moments after kissing you?"

"I don't think..." she started out.

"What do you have to lose? If things work out, you and Rian marry and live happily ever after. If you decide to walk away, then at least you will have shown my grandson what a fool he was to lose such a brilliant woman."

Amilee laughed, thinking that Inis was far more diabolical than anyone gave her credit for.

"The hospital discussion board is not a joke, my dear. This is a sincere offer and I think that you have a few fantastic ideas on the various topics." She stood up, gathering her purse. "I'll send you the information on the other participants and will let them know that you are tentatively accepting my invitation. If you don't want to join us, then there's no harm done. No pressure at all!" she said as she swept out of the room as if she were thirty years younger.

Amilee stared at the closed door, wondering what Inis was up to. The invitation to participate in the discussion group was truly an honor. And yes, she had a lot of ideas on treatment options that deviated from the old school methods. They weren't radical necessarily, but they were fresh and innovative.

Could she do it? Could she go back to Abidnae and participate in the hospital opening? It had been so long since she'd seen her father and she missed him very much. But how would Rian interpret her visit?

If she was clear about her reasons for accompanying him to Abidnae, perhaps he wouldn't apply additional meaning to her visit. Yes, she thought as she stood up and moved back to her desk to review the rest of her client files, she could do this. It would be a major coup for her career, something to put on her resume. And those kinds of discussion groups gave her an advantage in grant proposals and fellowship opportunities. She'd be a fool not to accept the invitation.

If only she could guarantee that Rian wouldn't misinterpret her reasons, she thought, tapping her pen thoughtfully against her chin as she stared out the window.

Chapter 10

Amilee dressed carefully that night, nervously smoothing a hand over her stomach as she gazed at her reflection in the mirror. She looked nothing like Razeen. There was a soft bump on her stomach and her breasts were too big, her hips wide, and…oh, what was the point?! She wasn't going to marry Rian, so why was she comparing herself to the woman who eventually would?

Just the thought of Razeen becoming Rian's wife sent a stab of jealousy shooting through her stomach.

"He's not yours!" she whispered, looking at herself in the mirror. That's when she saw the mark from last night. Straightening, she moved over to the closet and pulled out a scarf. Not the beautiful silk scarf that had arrived by special messenger earlier today. A different scarf. This one wasn't as nice, and it probably hadn't cost five hundred dollars, but would still serve its purpose. She twisted the ends into a sophisticated tie that looked…well, honestly, it looked odd. Unfortunately, there wasn't anything to do about the scarf. There was no way that she was going out in public with a hickey in plain view and she didn't have a wide variety of scarves or a dress with a high enough collar, that was also sufficiently fancy for where ever Rian would take her tonight.

"Jerk!" she muttered. The doorbell chimed and she muttered a curse as she rushed through her apartment, grabbing her evening purse and the tote that she normally used for work, stuffing her wallet, cell phone, lipstick, and keys into the smaller clutch, almost tripping over a pair of shoes before reaching the door.

Which was why she was slightly out of breath when she pulled the door open. And that was the reason she was a bit more irritated when she saw that he looked immaculately dressed, and not out of breath, as he stood looking down at her.

"We're not doing that again!" she stated, wanting that message to be loud and clear.

Rian's eyes widened briefly before his features softened with amusement. "We aren't?" he asked, reaching out to touch the scarf she'd just tied around her neck to cover the "that again" that they'd done last night.

"Nope. We're going out to dinner. I'm going to order something extravagant and expensive. You're going to select an excellent bottle of wine and then we're going to discuss how we're going to negate the terms of the betrothal contract."

With that statement made, she pulled her apartment door closed, tested the knob to make sure that the lock had caught, then looked up at him. Waiting.

"I see. That's quite the agenda you have planned," he replied, graciously extending his arm to her.

Amilee ignored his gesture, stepping around him. "This isn't a social evening. This is..." She'd been about to say that it was a business dinner, but he stopped her, pulling her back so she leaned against his chest.

"Don't try to ignore what happened between us last night, Amilee," he said softly, his lips perilously close to her ear. "Even now, I can feel your body trembling. I know that I pleasured you last night and I intend to show you more." He turned her to face him and kissed her softly before he pulled away. "And I can see the need in your eyes, my dear." With that, he took her hand and firmly placed it on his arm. Then he led her down the stairs to the parking lot, offering his hand to assist her into the waiting limousine.

Amilee gritted her teeth as she stepped into the limousine, looking up at the windows of her neighbors and praying that none of them happened to be watching. They'd be full of questions if she was seen getting into a limousine surrounded by large, intimidating men.

"You don't need to reveal your Neanderthal ways too early, Your..." She caught herself, looking over at him. Yep, the threat glowed in his eyes. Amilee gulped and mentally shook herself. "Rian," she corrected.

"You think I'm acting like a caveman when I want the woman I made love to over and over again last night to walk beside me? To acknowledge me?" He waited briefly before continuing. "Turn that question around. How would you feel if the roles were reversed? If we'd made love last night and the next day, I treated you as if you were invisible?"

Amilee's jaw dropped and her heart ached. She looked over at him, startled by what he was saying. "I didn't mean...I'm not trying to be cold hearted," she whispered, shifting so that she could more easily face him. "I just...I just feel like this whole situation is spinning out of control, Rian. I don't know how to handle it. You're...more than I realized. And..."

"And I terrify you," he supplied when she couldn't finish, struggling find the words to describe her feelings.

She shook her head, lowering her eyes slightly before looking out the window. "No. You don't terrify me. Not in that sense." She laughed, lifting a shoulder slightly. "Actually, yes, I guess you do. You do terrify me sexually, Rian. But not in the way you mean." She looked at him and couldn't stop the tears from welling up. "You scare me because I'm afraid that I'll get hurt. I try to come across as tough and confident, but deep down, I'm scared. Scared of everything that is expected of me, of the way that you can control me with just a kiss." She didn't add that she was terrified of falling in love with him, with the full knowledge that he could never fall in love with her. Amilee still remembered the stabbing pain as she'd watched Razeen drape herself against him.

"And if I promise never to intentionally hurt you?" he offered, his voice softer now.

She lifted her lashes, looking into his dark eyes. "What about unintentionally?"

The limousine pulled up outside of a well-known restaurant, his guards immediately opened the door. She stepped out, relieved that she'd dressed up for this dinner. It was a fancy place and, even though it was a weeknight, there was already a line of people waiting for tables and the bar was full.

Rian didn't wait though. Oh no! No waiting for a man of his exalted position. Or perhaps it was more about the security risks surrounding the presence of a world leader. Either way, Rian put a hand to the small of her back as he led her through the tables towards a private dining room in the back.

"This is nice," she said, her nervousness building as he held the chair out for her.

"You asked for dinner out," he replied, coming around to sit on the other side of the table.

"I understand that the food here is excellent."

Amilee's lips twitched with amusement. "Have you ever eaten a meal that wasn't perfectly prepared?"

He lowered his menu. "During desert training, the rations were about as far from 'perfectly prepared' as food could be. But the rations were nutritious, so I ate them."

Her eyes widened. "You went through desert training?"

"Of course. I've gone through all the various training offered by the Abidnae military, as well as training offered by other countries in specialized combat techniques."

"I read an article about the effects of the SERE training here in the United States. It sounds absolutely horrible." SERE was an acronym for "Survival, Evasion, Resistance, and Escape" training.

"It is," he replied, setting his menu down on the table beside him. "I went through it about five years ago and I can confirm that every moment of that training is possibly the worst thing any human could endure."

"It's astounding the things that human beings will put others through."

"You're right, but it is the world in which we live."

"Why would you go through such tortuous training?" she asked.

"Why wouldn't I?"

She stared at him, stunned and confused. "Because you're the leader of Abidnae. You are protected every moment of your life," she said, her gaze moving to each doorway where she knew guards were stationed.

"That's true, but what would happen if I ever were captured? If I hadn't gone through that kind of training, the knowledge that I have of my government's missions would be in jeopardy. It is essential that I go through the training, in order to protect every citizen in our country."

Amilee had to admire his sentiment, even if she didn't like the thought of him going through that kind of torture. "I don't believe that all world leaders go through that course. Could you imagine some of them enduring the trials of SERE training?"

They both shook their heads and Amilee felt a moment of camaraderie. It was very nice and she felt...odd.

"I know that you can't tell me the specifics about your job or the issues your patients have, but can you tell me a bit about what you do? What your day was like?"

She blushed and looked down at her lap, remembering the redness that was still an issue on her inner thighs. She'd worn stockings tonight because allowing her thighs to touch in any way was simply not an option.

"What just went through your mind?" he asked, seeing her blush.

"Nothing," she replied quickly, picking up her glass of ice water. "I just...Rebecca, the receptionist saw the dark mark on my neck before I realized it was there. And before...oh, by the way, the scarf that your assistant sent over was lovely. Thank you."

"You're welcome. I thought that the pink would look very nice with your outfit and complexion."

She stopped, staring across the table at him. "You didn't actually choose the scarf yourself, did you?" Surely not.

His eyes captured hers as he responded, "I *personally* selected the scarf,

Amilee. I know that some of my gifts to you in the past were disappointing. They were impersonal and lacked thought and care. I will do better in the future."

Oh, how surprisingly sweet of him! She couldn't handle the warmth that washed over her and had to look down at her lap to hide her expression, nervously smoothing the linen napkin. "Your gifts were always very nice," she replied, not wanting him to think her ungrateful.

"That locket that I gave to you for your fifteenth birthday?"

"Fourteenth," she corrected, remembering the disappointment as she'd realized that he didn't know what was in the box either.

"I know you hadn't liked it. And the pearls on your sixteenth birthday? They were trite. I would have selected something a bit more... daring or at least original. Pearls on a woman's sixteenth birthday felt lacking in creativity."

"Why didn't you?" she asked, curiously.

"I was told that you wouldn't have liked my gifts. That they weren't appropriate."

Her heart melted. "What were they?"

He rubbed a hand over the back of his neck, looking endearingly gruff and uncomfortable. She suspected that Rian rarely felt uncomfortable.

"Books. I remember our first conversation. You were talking about women in history and how women's contributions weren't often recognized. I'd gotten a book for you on women in history. But the person in charge of those things had carefully explained that girls of your age didn't like reading dry, boring books about history. They didn't like to read at all, unless it was about fashion, makeup, or movie stars."

"Oh," was all she could say. She really would have loved the book. She would have enjoyed anything that he'd chosen for her and not some faceless person who didn't know anything about her. "Well, I read the book you gave me several years later!" She smiled, trying to come up with something positive. "That's all in the past now. And thank you, again, for the scarf."

"I noticed over the years that you've never given me a gift," he commented.

Amilee nodded. "I know. And the fact that I haven't is a significant issue. My apologies. But in my defense, I was never invited to any of your birthday parties."

He chuckled. "And yet, you were forced to come to the palace every year for your birthday in order to allow me to celebrate with you."

She smiled. "I imagine that you were put out by having to attend those silly birthday dinners in my honor."

"I didn't mind."

She snorted. "Please! I was just one more obligation to you. I know what your days and evenings, probably most of your nights, are like, Rian. You're an incredibly busy man. You have too many obligations. My father used to tell me about your days and the issues that you dealt with." He looked worried, but she shook her head. "He never revealed anything he shouldn't have about your decisions," Amilee assured him immediately. "He merely explained the broad strokes of your life, to give me insight into what you have to deal with every day so I knew not to expect too much from you after our wedding." She twirled her glass of wine. "It was his way of preparing me for my future life." When she lifted her eyes, she shrugged. "My mother struggled to deal with my father's career. He made it home for dinner perhaps once a week. The rest of the time, he was either with your father or with you, or he was working at his office. We never knew if he'd be home or even if he was alive." She sighed. "I know that my father's job is very dangerous. Which is probably why he wanted me to understand your world."

"That's true enough," Rian agreed. The waiter arrived and they put in their orders, then eagerly turned back to each other, leaning forward with their elbows resting in the table as they continued the conversation. Amilee was amazed at some of the issues Rian revealed to her, and was touched by other stories. She especially liked the fact that he'd wanted to buy her something non-generic for her birthdays. It made him more...human.

Unfortunately, after they'd finished the lovely meal and had even shared a dessert and sweet port, Rian's assistant stepped into the room. "I'm terribly sorry to interrupt, Your Highness," the man murmured, bowing slightly. "But an urgent issue has come up that needs your attention."

Rian nodded sharply to the man, but Amilee noticed that he was gritting his teeth. Frustration?

"I'll just catch a cab home," she told him, picking up her purse, tucking it under her arm, and heading towards the door.

"Oh no, you won't!" he commanded, grabbing her elbow and swinging her around so she landed against his hard chest. "Come back with me," he urged. "Whatever the issue is, it won't take long to resolve and then we can enjoy the rest of this evening."

Amilee was so surprised by his urgency that, for a moment, she actually considered staying. But then her brain kicked back into gear and she shook her head, patting his chest lightly. "I don't think so. I think–"

He kissed her, stopping her next words. Again, Amilee was nearly swamped with lust, obliterating common sense.

When he lifted his head this time, she was breathing heavily. Thankfully, she noticed that he was too. That soothed her a little, although she still pulled away. "I need to go," she told him firmly.

"Amilee, we need to talk. Come back with me."

She shook her head. "I can't, Rian," she told him firmly, pulling herself together. "I'm traveling back to Abidnae this weekend though." She caught the gleam in his eyes and laughed softly. "Not for you. This is for me. There's a–"

"Hospital opening. I know." He sighed, rubbing a hand across his jawline. "Fine. We will continue this conversation on the flight back to Abidnae. I'll pick you up tomorrow morning."

She smiled gently. "I'm not leaving tomorrow. I have three clients in the morning. So why don't you fly home and then I'll...."

Rian laughed, shaking his head. "You don't understand, but you will," he warned. "We'll shift our departure to after lunch. If you have any afternoon clients, please cancel them. It is too dangerous for you, and most likely for the people on a plane with you, for you to fly commercially. Not anymore." He lifted his cell phone and started speaking before she could question his comment. Dangerous? For her to fly? What in the world was he talking about?

He ended the call and took her hand, kissing her fingertips. "Your guards will ensure that you get home safely tonight. But it would be better if you came back to my penthouse with me. It would be easier for your guards to protect you there."

Amilee shook her head, confused. "Rian, there's really no need for your guards to stay with me. I can–"

He sighed and pulled her closer. "Amilee, you are my fiancée. People have seen you with me tonight and they will have made the connection. In the past, we were able to keep your identity more of a secret but now, things have been put into motion and your connection to me puts you in danger. It also puts others in danger. So please, allow my guards to get you home. Follow their instructions. Once we get back to Abidnae, then we can talk more about security issues and figure out a plan. Okay?"

Amilee wasn't sure she agreed, but she understood his point. So instead of arguing, she nodded. "Fine. But I'm not staying with you. I'm going home to my apartment. I'll see you tomorrow."

And with that, she walked out, watching him out of the corner of her eye to make sure he didn't try to pull her back into his arms and kiss her silly. As a means of control, it was powerful. But that didn't mean she liked it.

As she walked through the restaurant, she could feel two men, his guards, trailing after her. Amilee didn't know what to do about them so she simply continued walking. She wasn't going to bother asking them to drive her back to her apartment, but she wasn't sure what the protocol was for bodyguards in cab rides home.

She stepped out of the restaurant and lifted her hand, but one of the guards stepped forward just as a big, black SUV pulled up to the curb. "This way, ma'am," the guard said, opening the door for her.

"I don't…"

"Please, ma'am," he insisted, his sunglasses hiding his eyes, but she could tell that he was looking around, concerned about her being on the sidewalk and out in the open. "It's safer this way."

Amilee sighed, looked around but felt as if she were creating a scene. Several other people were waiting on the sidewalk, waiting for a table and they were watching curiously. So, she stepped into the back and the door closed.

Chapter 11

Amilee glared at the beautiful plane, wishing that she didn't have to climb those stairs and face him again. Not after a sleepless night. Her body was primed for the man and she was fairly certain that, as soon as he saw her, he'd know exactly why she was in such a foul mood.

"It's not going to take off without you," a deep voice came from beside her.

Amilee jumped about a foot, and glared at Rian. "Where...how did you...?" She stopped when his dark eyebrow lifted in question. "Never mind," she finished.

He laughed softly, sending shivers of awareness throughout her system. "I just got here. My car was right behind yours as we pulled through security at the gate. Are you ready?"

She sighed, shrugging slightly. "I guess so."

He wrapped an arm around her waist. "My grandmother is already on board. So, you'll be safely chaperoned." He paused, looking down at her. "Should I have come to your apartment last night?" he asked, his voice gentle as his eyes surveyed the shadows under her eyes. "You didn't sleep well, did you?"

"No," she admitted. "And I doubt your presence would have helped me sleep." She was stiff, praying that he didn't somehow sense the wildly naughty thoughts that had flitted through her mind all night.

"You can sleep on the flight," he promised. "Are you hungry? Did you eat lunch?"

"I'm not hungry," she told him, although she'd been too tired to make breakfast and hadn't bothered with lunch either. She'd been too nervous about seeing him again to eat anything. Plus, she'd been running behind on her schedule. Again

"Will you join me and my grandmother for lunch anyway?" he asked, taking her hand and tucking it onto his elbow as he led her towards the plane.

"I need to get my suitcase," she said, pulling back.

"The staff will get it," he assured her. "They'll also park your vehicle for you and bring you the keys if you give them to him."

"Thank you," she said to the man who was hurrying over to her. She handed over her keys and he nodded his thanks, rushing away.

"I'm not very good about releasing control," she grumbled as she walked towards the stairs to the plane.

"I've gathered that," he replied with a tone that implied he was amused. "Why is that?"

"Because I prefer being in control. Don't you?"

"Of course, but there are some things that we don't need control over. Such as carrying one's suitcase."

She sighed, turning as she stood on the first step of the stairs. She was at his eye level now and she looked directly at him. "I suppose that wanting to be in control of my suitcase has something to do with the fact that I feel as if I'm losing control of so many other aspects of my life. Such as this weekend. And this betrothal. And every time you kiss me, you're trying to control me. Don't think I haven't noticed. It's really irritating, by the way." She paused in order to shoot a fulminating glare at him, but he merely chuckled at her ire.

With exasperation thrumming through her veins, Amilee turned and preceded him up the stairs, wishing that she could say more. Unfortunately, she didn't have the words. In his mind, there wasn't anything wrong with a betrothal to a stranger. He'd just take it in stride, as if marrying someone and becoming intimate with a stranger was a non-issue. But he had control over other aspects of his life. He wasn't in jeopardy of getting his heart wounded, again. He'd never kissed her, then seen her walk over to another man and kiss him!

Nor would he, because Amilee just wasn't like that. She had no idea how to flirt. Which wasn't really the point, she told herself as she looked around, spotting Inis sitting by one of the windows.

Amilee headed towards her and Inis looked up, smiling warmly at her. "Dear, it's...!"

"Excuse us for just a moment, Grandmother."

Strong fingers grabbed Amilee's arm and she was practically dragged away from the main area of the plane towards the back. It was quieter here, more private. Amilee jerked her arm out of Rian's grip and swung around, furious.

"Just what the hell do you think...!"

He kissed her. Amilee was so angry, she pushed against his chest, shoving him back, but he merely followed her, his eyes burning with that desire that always simmered just under the surface with him.

"You said I could control you with just a kiss," he growled, making her walk backwards until her back was against the wall.

"I didn't mean it as a good thing!" she hissed out, still pushing against him, but he was too big.

"Show me!" he replied, his hands hot on her waist, then sliding higher. "I want to see you lose control when I kiss you!"

"No!" she snapped back. "I don't–"

If he'd kissed her hard, then she might have been able to resist him. But this was a slow, gentle, nibbling kiss. Amilee was lost. Tilting her head backwards, she let him kiss her, returning the caress as she lifted her hands to rest against his chest. When he deepened the kiss, Amilee's hands slid higher, wrapping around his neck.

When he straightened, he shook his head. "You don't understand something important, Amilee," he said, his voice hoarse.

"What's that?"

"You have the same power over me."

With that, he stepped back, taking her hand. "As much as I'd like to continue this, we need to sit down so the pilot can take off. Also, my grandmother hasn't eaten yet today. As soon as we get into the air, I want the flight crew to serve lunch. You don't mind sitting with us, do you? I know that my grandmother likes you. She's asked about you often over the years and asked me several times today to make sure that you was coming with us."

Amilee's heart warmed. The elderly woman was very sweet and had been by Amilee's side during some of the most painful moments of her life. She was the grandmother Amilee never had, and the mother Amilee wished for.

"Of course I'll sit with her," she said, pointedly referring to Inis and not the man who made her turn all mushy. "And I'd love a meal. I didn't have a chance to grab anything after my last client today."

"Good," he replied, taking her hand and leading her back to the main cabin where they both sat down in front of Inis.

As soon as they were seated and buckled up, the plane shifted forward, preparing for takeoff.

Amilee listened with half an ear as Rian and Inis discussed the hospital opening and the various events that would take place to celebrate the momentous occasion. But she couldn't stop thinking about what Rian had just told her. She had the same power over him? Could she truly distract him the way he did her?

He only kissed her silly when he didn't want to hear what she had to say. Or if he disagreed with her. Or if she wasn't complying with whatever edict he'd just laid down. It was such an intriguing thought, she couldn't focus on the conversation.

One of the flight attendants brought them lunch and Amilee ate it. She knew that it smelled delicious, but when the flight attendant came by to take their plates away, she couldn't remember what she'd eaten.

Glancing at the two of them, she noticed several curious glances from Rian and…was that a smug expression on Inis features? Yes, it was! Amilee squirmed in her seat, not sure what that look was about. Had she been lured to Abidnae on false purposes?

No, Inis wouldn't do that!

Would she?

The woman was wily enough. So maybe. Then again, they'd been discussing the hospital opening.

Amilee shook her head, wondering if she was going nuts. Inis couldn't have invented a hospital opening like this. It took years to plan, develop, build, and hire staff for a hospital! One couldn't do it overnight. Not even someone as amazing as Inis.

So what was going on?

"You're quiet," Rian commented. "What's going through your mind?"

Amilee shook her head, pushing her glasses higher onto her nose. "Just tossing things around in my head, trying to make sense of everything." Unfortunately, Inis and Rian had excellent poker faces. Interesting, she thought, wondering if she'd ever be that good at hiding her emotions and thoughts.

"What doesn't make sense?" he asked.

Amilee shook her head. "I don't know. There are a lot of changes happening right now. It's difficult to process."

Inis stood up, smiling at them. "I'm going to go take a nap, my dears. You two have a great deal to talk about and you don't need an old lady eavesdropping."

Rian watched his grandmother walk away, concerned. "Is she walking more slowly than normal?" he asked.

He felt Amilee turn her head. Rian was always amazed at how he was completely aware of everything Amilee did. Every part of her body, every movement, gesture, and twitch to her features, he took in on different levels. He liked to just sit back and watch her, to see the emotions flit across her face. But he was also aware of how she wanted to hide those emotions from him.

Rian understood, to a point. Years ago, they'd been trapped by the betrothal contract. At twenty, he hadn't really cared who he would marry. Besides, Amilee had been a pretty child with the promise of growing into a lovely woman. He hadn't minded becoming betrothed to her, especially after he'd learned that she wasn't a silly child without ambition.

Now, he was aware that her career ambitions might hinder her happiness in their marriage. A marriage that he was very much looking forward to. So, how could he help her anticipate their wedding with as much hope and eagerness as he did? He gazed down at her, noticed her hands were tightly clasped in her lap. Amilee was still watching his grandmother's slow steps until Inis closed the door that led to the private bedrooms at the back of the plane.

He heard her sigh, but she was still tense, her shoulders tight and her hands still clasped tightly together.

"Talk to me, Amilee. Tell me what's bothering you."

Amilee forced a smile. "What time will we land?"

He wanted to talk, to discuss her concerns. But the look in her eyes warned him that she wasn't ready to have that conversation. Not yet. He told her the time and she nodded.

"Good, that gives me most of the afternoon to review client files," she told him, grabbing her bag and moving to the other side of the plane to read the files she'd brought with her.

Rian watched her, fighting down a chuckle as she pushed those cute glasses higher up onto the bridge of her nose. She had no idea what a temptation she was. Her eyes were dark and mysterious, her long, raven hair a sensuous delight. Not to mention, she had the cutest nose and…okay, the glasses were sexy too. Then there were her breasts. Her figure was the stuff men dreamed of. He remembered holding her in his arms and her soft, curvy body fit against his perfectly.

And yet, he also enjoyed talking with her, just being with her. That was such a strange sensation that he wasn't sure what it meant. Women…he usually didn't connect with them the way he did with Amilee. What was it about her?

Just to confirm that she felt the connection just as he did, she turned her head and glared at him, letting him know that she didn't appreciate his staring.

Rian chuckled and looked away, wondering where his assistant had gone. Didn't the man have a stack of issues for him to review? Even as he thought it, the man appeared, carrying the leather portfolio stuffed with papers.

"Your Highness, we have…" and so it began. The man sat down across from Rian, going through each of the documents and pointing to the required signature spaces. For the first time in his life, Rian couldn't focus. And that was completely because of Amilee. He could feel the weight of her gaze on him, although he kept his attention on his assistant or the papers in front of him.

Interesting, he thought as he put his signature to yet another document. She could feign indifference most of the time. But not always. And not when he touched her. Damn, he liked that!

Chapter 12

Amilee's cheeks hurt. She'd greeted so many people and couldn't remember a single name. The hospital opening had been a spectacular success, with hundreds of families bringing their kids to update their vaccinations, many of the kids even going through a quick exam with a pediatrician. Hundreds of adults had signed up to get an annual exam and they were intrigued by the wellness possibilities the hospital would offer throughout the year.

The only downside was that Rian had commanded that she sit with him on the dais. Her presence here made it seem as if their relationship was more formalized than it actually was. She didn't like that, but because there had been too many reporters around when he'd whispered in her ear, she hadn't been able to argue with him.

So here she stood, shaking hands and nodding greetings as if she knew who each person was and why they were here. Rian was doing the same thing, but he seemed to handle the crowds more efficiently. He also seemed to know people's names and their importance within the government.

She was so tired. Down to her very bones exhausted. And more than slightly disappointed, but she'd never admit that she'd hoped Rian would come to her last night. At first, she'd lain awake, angry because she'd expected Rian to come. She'd told herself that she didn't want him there, that she wanted him to respect her and not invade her privacy. But, by the time midnight rolled around, and he still hadn't even knocked on her door to say goodnight, she was furious. Didn't he want her anymore? Was she just a one night stand to him? He'd gotten what he wanted and now, he didn't want her anymore?

Her palm itched to slap his handsome face. And yet, Amilee knew she was being completely irrational!

"Ready to go?" he asked, whispering in her ear.

Amilee jerked, her eyes angry until she realized how close he was. Her eyes dropped to his mouth, her body almost leaning towards him.

He growled, pulling her against his side as he nodded to his guards. "We need to get out of here," he told the lead guard. The man immediately started towards the door, politely telling the others waiting for "just a word" with Rian or Amilee, that they had another engagement.

Amilee had no idea what the urgency was about, but she was relieved not to have to keep smiling and nodding. She was also gratified that her comments on the discussion panel had been well received, but she was exhausted, both mentally and physically. All she wanted to do was soak in a hot bath and take a nap before the big gala tonight.

Just thinking about tonight made her head ache and she dove into the waiting SUV with relief.

"Thank you," she whispered to Rian as he sat next to her. Leaning her head back against the cushions, she closed her eyes and tried to relax. "All those people seemed to think I should know who they were. And when they realized I didn't have a clue, they'd introduce themselves, then wait expectantly, as if their names should be significant to me." She rubbed her temples. "That was exhausting."

He pulled her closer, settling her against his chest. Amilee knew she should protest, but he pressed his thumbs into the tight muscles of her shoulders and she melted in his hands. "Oh, that feels wonderful!" she sighed.

"Why are you so tense?" he asked, his warm breath teasing the hair by her ear.

"I'm always tense when I have to talk in front of people. And then you asked me to sit on the stage, where I had to stare out at all of those curious faces." She smiled crookedly. "Do you know how hard it is to cross one's legs at the ankles? If I'd known that I was going to be on stage like that, I would have worn slacks."

"But you have great legs. Why would you cover them up with slacks?"

She chuckled. "Because I'm up on stage! My skirt doesn't reach my knees, so if I crossed my legs, even a little, I'd end up flashing the audience." She glanced over her shoulder at him. "That's not something that men ever have to worry about. It's yet another injustice that women have to endure." She said that last with a teasing tone, but her point was valid. It was damned uncomfortable to sit on a stage and not move for fear that one's skirt might gape. She supposed that's why so many female political figures wore black panties. It was hard to distinguish one's panties from a shadow. In her case though, she hadn't considered the potential for on-stage flashing, so she'd worn her regular, white cotton panties.

"I'm sorry the world is so unfair."

She shrugged, grumbling a bit more. "Well, men have to kill all the spiders."

He laughed again. "I suppose there are compensations for the hurdles women have to deal with."

"You're making fun of me."

He bent, kissing her neck. "You're right. I am. What are you going to do about it?"

She laughed softly, pulling away so that she was sitting beside him. "I'm not going to do anything about it because you would enjoy my wrath too much."

He threw back his head, laughing at her quip. "You're probably right."

"Why is that?" she asked, tilting her head quizzically.

He reached out and took her hand, lifting it up so that he could press kisses to her fingers. "Perhaps because any reaction from you is worthwhile. It reminds me that you're not as oblivious to me as you pretend."

"I'm not oblivious at all. Unfortunately." She saw the heat building in his eyes and pulled her hand away. "I shouldn't have said that. Now you're going to..."

He reached out and lifted her into his arms, settling her on his lap. "I'm going to what?" he asked, his hand sliding down her thigh.

"You're going to..." she stopped, words caught in her throat as his hand slid under her skirt. "Rian!"

He watched her face while his hand inched higher. "Why are you so tired?"

"Because..."

"Is it because you were waiting for me last night?

"You wish!" she gasped, grabbing his hand, but there was no strength in her grip and his hand inched higher. And higher!

"We can't...not here!" she hissed, closing her eyes at the heat stealing up through her body.

"You're right," agreed, lowering his head to kiss her neck. "We will be at the palace in less than three minutes." He nipped at her earlobe. "I'm hoping to convince you to take a nap with me."

"A nap?"

His hand continued to slide along her thigh, making rational thought impossible. "Yes. A nap. In my bed. Alone. Without anyone to stop me from exploring every inch of you."

Amilee shivered, wanting that too. But in the back of her mind, a warning bell sounded.

"Stop thinking, Amilee," he coaxed. "Just feel."

Unfortunately, the limousine pulled into an underground parking garage. The abrupt transition from bright sunlight to darkness startled Amilee. She opened her eyes and looked around. "Oh!" she gasped and slid off of Rian's lap as the driver pulled up beside the palace elevator and another guard stepped up to open the door.

Rian stepped out first, then extended his hand to Amilee. For a long moment, she hesitated to accept his help, but in the end, she didn't really have a choice. So, she extended her shaking fingers to him, almost relieved when his strong hand wrapped around her smaller one, balancing her as she stepped out of the vehicle.

"This way," he told her, leading her towards the elevator. Thankfully, several bodyguards entered the elevator as well, surrounding them. Amilee breathed a sigh of relief, even though her body protested the withdrawal of his touch.

As soon as the elevator doors opened up, Rian's assistant came into view. It was obvious that the man wanted to discuss something with Rian, and Amilee smiled brightly, feeling pleased at somehow thwarting Rian's seduction.

"I'll see you tonight at dinner," she told him, shooting an amused glance over her shoulder as she continued down the hallway.

Rian watched as Amilee sauntered away, his body tight and desperate for her. Of course, she thought she'd escaped him. Little did she know that the look she'd thrown his way had ignited his predator instincts. She wanted him to chase her? He was going to chase her until she was screaming his name with pleasure.

His assistant continued to natter about... whatever it was, but Rian wasn't listening. In fact, he lifted a hand, silencing his assistant as he watched Amilee turn the corner, heading towards her suite.

He knew that she thought she'd gotten away from him. But that look, that challenging glance called to him. Dared him! And he wasn't a man to ignore a challenge.

"We'll have to discuss this later," he told his assistant, unwilling to wait until tonight to respond to her challenge.

Chapter 13

Rian knocked on the door, but didn't get an answer.

"She's in her suite?" he asked one of her personal bodyguards. Amilee didn't grasp that the men and women standing outside of her doorway were her permanent team. He suspected that she thought they were just watching out for her while she was in the palace.

"Yes, Your Highness," the man on the right replied. "She entered about fifteen minutes ago."

Rian nodded and pushed the door open. Silence.

Then there was a small squeaking noise and the sound of water splashing. "Bath time?" he asked, moving towards the large bathroom.

Sure enough, as soon as he stepped into the steam-filled bathroom, he spotted Amilee leaning her head back against a rolled up towel, the bath filled with lavender scented suds.

Her hair was piled on top of her head and she was bouncing to the music coming through her headphones. Walking over to her, he moved to the opposite side of the tub, watching to see how long it would take for her to realize that he was there.

As he watched, one of her toes appeared through the suds, tapping along to the beat in her ears. Rian thought she was adorably sexy, even if a part of him was annoyed with her for being completely unaware of someone in her bathroom. He made a mental note to increase the guards on her team. If she was this unaware, he would do what needed to be done to protect her.

Unbuttoning his shirt, he tossed it over the clothes she'd left piled on the counter, watching her the whole time. It was pretty shocking how important she'd become. She was like a stealth lover, inching into his psyche a little bit at a time, until Amilee was all he could think about.

He'd just tossed his slacks away when a sound must have filtered through the music because she opened her eyes, startled to find him stepping into the steamy water.

"What...!" she gasped, sitting up straighter as she pulled her ear buds out. "Rian! What are you doing?" she demanded, sliding across to the other side of the large tub.

"I'm taking you up on your invitation," he explained calmly, grabbing her foot when she tried to slip further away. With deft fingers, he pressed his thumbs against the arch of her foot. Initially, she tried to pull her foot away, but when he applied the pressure, she closed her eyes with a moan, leaning her head back slightly.

For several moments, there was silence as he continued to massage her feet. Then Amilee lifted her head back up and, searching for her glasses, again tried to pull her foot away. "What do you mean? I didn't invite you here!"

He laughed and reached down to take her other foot. "Of course you did," he argued, pressing his foot into the arch of her foot.

She moaned again, then shook her head. "I didn't."

"Sure you did." He pressed again, eliciting another groan, this time she had to reach out to steady herself before she slipped below the water's surface. "That look you sent to me before you walked away," he replied, continuing the massage. "It was definitely an invitation."

Amilee bit her lip in indecision. She wasn't sure if she wanted to pull her foot away and argue with him, or remain silent and enjoy his ministrations. She settled somewhere in the middle.

"That look wasn't an invitation, Rian. It was me walking away from you."

"It was a challenge, Amilee," he argued, as his fingers explored their way along her leg.

She opened her mouth to argue, but his hands moved higher. He loved that he could fluster her like this. But at the moment, he knew that her reaction was more than just being flustered. There was desire in her eyes. Desire, heat, and need.

Rian intended to satisfy every one of those needs. Many times over, he vowed.

Amilee gazed at Rian over the froth of bubbles, shocked and...okay, so maybe she had been secretly hoping that this would happen. Last night, she'd missed him. But...maybe she wasn't quite prepared for this.

"I think that the fantasy of you is quite different from the reality of you, Rian," she announced, her voice weak as she moved her foot away from his lap. "You're incredibly intimidating."

Rian's dark eyebrow quirked at that statement, then he scooted over to her side of the tub. "Amilee, talk to me. I'm not sure what you mean by that comment." He lifted her from the water, moving her so that she was sitting with her back against his chest, his impressive erection pressing against her back as well.

"You're…" her eyes fluttered closed as his hands slid over her outer thighs, straight down to her knees. But those hands didn't stop there. They moved higher, but this time, his fingers trailed along the soapy skin of her inner thighs. Amilee's body betrayed her, opening to him with every intimate foray closer and closer to parts of her that craved his touch.

"I want you, Amilee," he whispered into her ear, nipping at the lobe to reinforce his statement. "Tell me that you want me too."

"I do!" she replied, because there was nothing else she could say. It was the truth. She wanted him and…after missing him last night, she was terrified of what that meant. "But you're going to hurt me, Rian."

"I'm not going to hurt you, love," he promised. "I'll be gentle."

Amilee closed her eyes as the tears burned under her eyelids. He didn't understand, and her betraying body wasn't giving her the chance to make him understand. So instead, she shifted around so that she was straddling his lap, his hands moving her hips into place. He lifted her higher, his mouth latching onto one taut nipple and Amilee arched into him, feeling that touch in ways that seemed impossible! His strong hands held her still, pressed against her back as he moved to her other breast. It was too much and Amilee cried out, her body pressing against his lap until she felt that delicious pressure against her core. Slowly, she lowered herself down, loving the way he filled her up. She arched her back again, rolling her hips until she could take all of him. Then, she remained still, savoring this moment, reveling in the uniqueness of being so intimately connected to Rian!

"You gotta move, love!" he hissed, his hands stroking her back, which was slick from the water and bubbles.

"Just a moment," she breathed, adjusting their bodies a bit more. She smiled when she heard him groan again, feeling powerful. "Okay, now we can…"

Before she could finish, Rian lifted her into his arms, shifting their positions so that she was seated, barely, on the edge of the massive tub. As he slowly thrust into her, Amilee clung to him, not just because she worried about falling backwards onto the hard marble floor, but also because every thrust sent her pleasure spiraling higher and higher. She could barely manage to tell him that it felt wonderful. All she could do was cling to him, completely at his mercy. Thankfully, he held her safely in place as he shifted and thrust, building their pleasure higher and higher. Although it seemed impossible, every plunge into her body felt like he was touching her soul, every shift of his hips sent her pleasure coursing through her veins like fire. And when she reached that pinnacle, Amilee buried her face against his neck, almost sobbing as her release throbbed around them.

But the moment wasn't over. Rian waited only long enough for her to come to her release before he moved faster, harder, his body clamoring and…finally giving Amilee yet another, smaller, climax just as he reached his own pleasure, groaning into her hair as his breath tingled along her skin.

When he moved, bringing them back down into the water, Amilee still straddling his hips and the two of them intimately connected, Rian cradled her in his arms, kissing her shoulders and neck, her forehead and cheeks, everywhere he could reach.

"Are you okay?" he asked, his hands smoothing over her back.

Amilee tried to lift her head, to smile and show him she was fine. But she was limp. She could no more form words than she could pin him to a wall. Instead, she merely nodded, smiling dreamily against his neck.

She heard a grumbling and pretended that he was laughing with her. Goodness his hands felt so good against her back! Amilee wondered if she could go on like this, just like this, for the rest of her life!

Apparently, Rian had different ideas. He lifted her away, setting her on one of the contoured seats in the massive tub, and proceeded to lather her up from chin to toes. But he didn't simply lather her with soap, he brought her whole body to life all over again. But this time, he took his time. He lifted her out of the water, slowly, thoroughly dried her off with his hands and his mouth, then stood up and carried her to the huge bed, laying her down only to kiss every inch of her. By the time he entered her this time, she was a sobbing, desperate mess, clinging to him, needing him, demanding that he give her that pleasure all over again.

And when he did, she cried out with her pleasure, tightening every muscle in her body to increase his pleasure and smiling when he collapsed against her, both of them replete and struggling for breath.

Chapter 14

Rian pushed through the doors of the private living room and walked directly to the bar. Pouring himself a large glass of scotch, he gazed at the crystal glass, watching the light filter through it a moment before he downed the spirit in one gulp. Hissing as the liquid burned down his throat, he slammed the glass down, surprised that it didn't shatter upon impact.

"Something bothering you?"

Rian swung around, searching for the voice. When he found his grandmother sitting on a chair with her sewing, his shoulders relaxed. "I didn't know you were in here," he explained, and turned away to pour himself another glass of the scotch.

"Obviously, dear," Inis replied gently. "Come. Sit down and tell me what is so bad that you have resorted to scotch at ten o'clock in the morning."

He stopped and blinked at her, stunned to realize that it was so early. Looking out the window, he didn't see the orchard of fruit trees or the blazing sun. All he could see was Amilee.

For the past two weeks, he'd made love to her, became intoxicated by the way she offered her body to him without reserve. Every night, he came to her room and she welcomed him with open arms. But by morning, she was gone, off doing...whatever the hell she did during the day. In other words, Amilee freely gave him her body, but she held everything else back.

Staring down at the alcohol in the cut crystal glass, he wondered what he was doing wrong. Why did she hold everything else back? And why the hell couldn't he get her out of his mind! She'd smile at him, and he became a blithering idiot. She argued with him over dinner and he had no idea what he'd eaten. Even thinking about those gorgeous hands of hers, and he was lost to everything but the glow he felt at her touch!

And yet, anytime he wanted to discuss making their relationship permanent, to set a date for their wedding, he couldn't find her.

It was almost as if she knew exactly when he wanted to talk and purposely hid away!

He glared down at the drink in his hand, berating himself for reaching for a crutch. But he didn't pour the scotch back into the decanter. Instead, he carried it with him as he sat down across from his grandmother. "What are you working on?" he asked, referring to the embroidery on her lap.

"Oh pish, dear," Inis scoffed. "Stop stalling. You've become such a private person that you don't feel as if you can confide in anyone." Her gaze gentled as she continued. "Which is wrong, my dear. There are at least two people that you could confide in, if you were only willing to trust us."

He chuckled. "I know that I can talk to you, Grandmother. I just..." he stopped, his eyes focusing on her. "Who is the other person?"

She smiled gently. "Why, Amilee of course."

He muttered another curse and stood up, unable to be still with such thoughts whirling through his head. "You know that's not true, Grandmother." Hell, he couldn't even find her, most of the time! If he could, he would have set a wedding date by now!

"I know it *is* true. And you're a blind fool, my dear."

He stopped pacing to look over at her, startled by her harsh words. "Why am I a fool?"

She smiled, shaking her head. "Tell me what is bothering you first."

"Amilee!" he growled. "She's...frustrating!"

His grandmother offered him a knowing smile. "Most women are, darling. But can you be a bit more specific?"

"She...!" he started off, throwing his hand in the air only to let it drop to his side. "She gives me only a small part of herself," he explained carefully. "And yet, I can't figure out how to convince her that I want all of her."

Inis smiled, her head tilting to the side as she watched him carefully. "You're in love with her, aren't you, my dear?"

He snorted. "Love! This has nothing to do with love, Grandmother. This is about my future with Amilee. And the future of Abidnae!" He grumbled as he continued to pace, his drink forgotten as he tried to make sense of it all. "This is important. I need to finalize this issue and I can't afford to bring fantasy emotions into the mix." He took a sip of the scotch, then resumed his pacing. "She's just so...standoffish about some things, but then she'll talk to me about something and I'll feel as if she's accepted me, that we could finally set the date and move forward. But then she pulls back, her eyes look at me as if..." he sighed heavily, rubbing a hand over his face as the weariness and confusion threatened to overwhelmed him. "As if I'm some sort of serial killer."

Inis shook her head. "You think love is a fantasy? That it isn't real?"

Rian shrugged as he glared at his sweet, if slightly delusional, grandmother. "You're missing the point. I don't give a damn about love. I want to finish this thing between Amilee and I! But in answer to your question, I know that some people believe in love. I don't."

"Well," she replied with sadness dimming her gaze. "First of all, I do believe in love. I felt a very deep love for your grandfather. He was the love of my life, the man who made my heart jump every time he stepped into the room." She sighed heavily. "I also think that your misunderstanding of love is one of your problems."

"One?" he snorted. "So you're saying that, if I believed in love, then she'd accept me and we could get married? Move on and figure out a life together?"

She laughed softly. "Oh, no. There are a few other issues you'd need to resolve before that can happen. But believing in this mysterious and confusing, sometimes confounding emotion is a good first step."

Rian groaned and braced his hands on the back of the sofa facing her. "I don't suppose you have some sort of road map that could help me?"

Inis chortled, shaking her head. "Oh, my dear, you are in deeper trouble than I realized. How has it come to pass that you don't believe in love? Or that you don't know the way to a woman's heart? You have no idea the kinds of things that could break that tender heart?" Her eyes turned speculative. "Or perhaps it would be more accurate to say her heart is closed off specifically to *you*."

"Closed off?" he snapped, staring at his grandmother. He wasn't sure if he should be angry or curious. He couldn't think of anything that he'd done or said to Amilee that would cause her pain.

Had he?

"Why would Amilee be closed off to me specifically?"

She looked at him curiously. "Let's start with the first question," she said. Inis ignored his sigh of frustration and continued. "Explain to me why you think that love is a fantasy?"

He snorted his disgust. "Isn't love just an easy way to justify one's lust?" he asked, not bothering to temper his words. She'd started the conversation, she could handle earthy responses. "Love is a way for two people who need some way to justify a sexual relationship. They need pretty words to make their desires feel justified. But in reality, it's all the same thing. Lust, passion, desire...whatever you want to call it, sex is a basic human need and we shouldn't have to wrap it in a pretty bow to enjoy it."

He waited, wondering how his grandmother would take his explanation. Would she be offended by his words or the sentiment behind them? But she'd lived in this world for over seventy-five years and had been married to Rian's grandfather for more than forty of those years. So, she knew the ins and outs of marriage. He doubted he could shock her.

Unfortunately, he wasn't prepared for her to shock him!

With her hands primly folded on her lap, she gazed up at him with a knowing smile. "You love her!" his grandmother whispered. "You're in love with Amilee!"

Rian blinked at her for a long moment, stunned and...angry? No, not angry. Confused. A moment later, he barked with shocked amusement. "Grandmother, where do you get these ridiculous notions?"

She laughed, slapping her knee in merriment. "Oh, this is delightful! You have fallen in love with the woman who has led you quite a merry chase over the years, haven't you?"

His amusement evaporated. "No!" he replied sharply. "I don't believe in love, Grandmother. Love is for poets and saps who need to–"

"I know," she interrupted, waving away his denial. "People who need to 'justify' a sexual relationship." She snorted her disagreement. "Let me ask you a few questions, my dear."

"Go ahead," he replied, pacing again.

"Do you enjoy her company?"

He stopped. "Yes. Of course. She's an intelligent, well-read, thoughtful individual who is genuinely interesting to converse with. I respect her opinions." He shrugged slightly. "That's not love, Grandmother. That's respect."

She smiled, nodding her head. "You're right. Enjoying a conversation with someone isn't love. But that's not what I'm asking you, dear. Do you enjoy *her*? When you aren't with her, do you think about her? Do you specifically seek out her company?"

Rian thought about it for a long moment. *Was* there something special about Amilee? Yes, of course. She was his fiancée. Of course she was special to him.

But was there more? He thought about the eagerness with which he'd always waited for her arrival each year. He remembered going over their conversations long after her birthday celebrations had passed. He knew he'd mentally replayed their conversations more than once, coming up with ideas for presents that she might like. Whenever he'd met another woman, he'd compared her to Amilee. And those ladies always fell short.

Rian looked at his grandmother, recognizing the understanding and compassion in her eyes. Sighing, he rubbed the back of his neck as his frustration built. "Yes. I do enjoy her company. Even when we're not talking, I like being with her. She's..." he hunted for the right word, but nothing came to mind to describe how he felt when he was around her. He thought "comforting" was what he was trying to say, but there was no way that Amilee's presence could be considered comforting. Just the opposite. When he saw her, he wanted to rip her clothes off and make love to her until she screamed his name. And yet, there were those times when he simply held her. He could have gone to his own bed after making love to Amilee, but he enjoyed holding her, feeling her cuddle against him. He didn't like waking up without her in his arms. He even looked for her, seeking her out when he...when he what? When he just wanted to see her?

"I see your feelings for Amilee are more complex than simple respect," his grandmother said, interrupting his contemplation.

Rian blinked, trying to shake off the odd feeling that he was missing something. Something important. "What of it?" he demanded. "Amilee is a beautiful woman. Who wouldn't want to spend time with her?"

Inis laughed, shaking her head. "So, you seek out her company. You..." she eyed him carefully, "...desire her." She smiled slightly. "Sometimes, that desire is a bit...distracting?" She waited for a moment, then laughed when he compressed his lips. "I'll take that as a yes. Plus, you not only want to spend the rest of your life with her, but you are eager to start that phase of your life, simply because you like the idea of her being by your side?"

His jaw tightened as he considered her words. Then he shook his head, rejecting her summary of the situation. "Yes. But that's not love that is..." he stopped, not sure how to define it. "That's accepting that our futures are intertwined and have been since we signed that betrothal contract."

She nodded, pursing her lips as she contemplated his response. "One last question."

"What is it?"

"Would you want to marry Amilee if you had never signed that betrothal contract?"

He blinked at his grandmother. He wanted to deny it. He wanted to tell her that he probably would have married another woman by now. But was that the truth? He remembered their interactions over the years with crystal clarity. If he hadn't met Amilee, hadn't grown into adulthood with that contract, where would he be now?

Would he have married someone else? He couldn't deny how impressed he'd been with her on that first day. She'd been only twelve years old and yet, she'd spoken to him with such...intelligence. Then on her fourteenth birthday, when she'd sat next to him outside in the courtyard discussing women's history...he'd been impressed. And the lust! Even at twenty, he'd felt lust for her. That had embarrassed him, infuriated him....but then the kiss that year in the courtyard...damn, that kiss had rocked his world!

Every time she'd been in the room, he'd felt it. He hadn't understood what 'it' was, but it had been floating around the two of them, drawing them together. Their eyes had always caught, even from across the room or the dining table.

What the hell was wrong with him? What had happened? Had she cast a spell over him? Had she...? He had no idea. Every option that came to mind seemed impossible.

Inis laughed softly, touching his hand to bring him back to the present. "It's called love, my dear boy. And it is one of the most powerful forces in the universe. It has altered the course of history too many times to count."

Rian looked up at her, still not believing in this love issue. "I don't–"

"You can deny it all you want. But Amilee is the woman you desire. She's the woman you seek out. She's the person you want to be with." She gave him a satisfied grin. "It's love, my dear. Pure love. And I'm thrilled that you've found this with your betrothed. Not everyone experiences that kind of pure love. It is a gift. You must not abuse it, Rian. And you must not abuse Amilee anymore by denying your love."

"I don't abuse women, Grandmother," he spat, outrage coloring his tone.

She looked up at him with compassion. "You don't hit them. That's for cowards!" she snorted. Her face cleared as she continued. "I'm talking about love, my dear. Love for the woman who makes you feel whole. Love for the woman you want to make happy."

That was true enough, he thought. Rian knew that he'd do anything to bring a smile to Amilee's face. He stopped pacing, his head spinning with unfamiliar ideas. Was this strange feeling he had towards Amilee...love? He'd scoffed at the very idea of love for so long, it was difficult to grasp the potential that he actually....maybe...perhaps...was in love?

He gazed at his grandmother. Still not sure, he shook off the confusion. "Okay, suppose that I do...love...her. What's the problem then?"

Inis laughed. "You really are completely unaware when it comes to women, aren't you?" He took a breath to argue with her, but she held up a hand. "No, I'm not talking about sexual exploits, my dear. I'm talking about women and what they need, what they want." She looked at him carefully. "What they truly desire."

Standing, she sighed and turned to him. "Give me your arm, dearest, and I will tell you a story as we walk."

Rian didn't want to hear a story. He didn't want to walk. But he'd never deny his grandmother anything. So instead of going in search of Amilee, he politely offered his arm. "Where are we going?"

"This way," and she led him through the glass doors that led out to the courtyard.

"Why are we walking in the garden, Grandmother?"

She patted his arm as they meandered along the moonlit paths. "I've loved this garden since I first arrived here to marry your grandfather. When I first moved here," she chuckled, "thousands of years ago, I wondered if perhaps the original owner of this palace had an ulterior motive in mind. The placement of this garden is really quite...extraordinary."

Rian looked around, noting the high walls that made it possible to secure the area from invaders. The tiled rooftop was also a good security measure. The tiles were difficult to walk on and noisy to boot. The pressure of a heavy footstep might even snap the tiles, which would alert the security guards that patrolled the area. He also knew that there were pressure sensors scattered among the rooftop tiles, along the edges, and in random patterns along the pathways.

"It's a solid structure," he finally agreed.

They reached the bench underneath the overhanging tree. The very bench where he'd found Amilee several times over the years. How many conversations had they shared on this bench? How many times had they laughed about something that had happened during the evening? He looked around, noting the tall glass doors surrounding the courtyard.

"I used to find Amilee out here fairly often. Her birthday dinners, her father's meetings, or for whatever reason," he commented. He smiled at the memories. "We used to sit here discussing politics while watching everyone inside."

"I've done that on several occasions," Inis agreed. "It's a strategic place for one to see what's going on inside, while the people inside are unaware that they are being watched."

Rian glanced at his grandmother. "And what have you seen out here?" he asked, amused. "Anything interesting?"

"Oh, you'd be surprised," she sighed, sitting down on the stone bench. "This used to be more comfortable, before age and frail bones started making life difficult for me." And yet, she sat down, shifting slightly as she stared into the now-dark glass doors. "The ballroom is through there," she pointed. "And over there," she said, pointing towards the right. "The billiards room is completely visible with the lights on inside."

Rian chuckled, thinking about the times he and his friends had slipped away to play billiards while some tedious event continued in the ballroom. "I remember beating my father several times at chess in that room. And all the conversations we had. He was teaching me strategy, helping me to grasp the complexities of every situation. There was never a single answer to a problem, he used to tell me as we stared at the chessboard. He wanted me to examine the problem from several angles."

"He was an intelligent man, my son." She shrugged her shoulders slightly. "My grandson..." she lifted her hand, wiggling it back and forth. "Can be a bit obtuse at times."

Rian narrowed his eyes at her. "What am I missing?" he demanded.

Inis patted his hand. "Did you know that Amilee is an introvert?"

He wasn't sure where this was going. "Yes, I had noticed. She can act extroverted for limited periods of time, but she used to come out here to hide from the crowds during the big events."

"Exactly. Amilee needs the quiet and stillness in order to regain her equilibrium. She'd come out here whenever she needed a break." She smiled softly. "I, too, am an introvert." She looked up at him now. "And, I believe that you are as well, but the demands of your role limit your ability to find peace and quiet. Am I right?"

"I suppose," he replied. He hadn't really thought about it in those terms. But he often found himself seeking out quiet places to contemplate difficult decisions.

"Amilee and I shared several special conversations out here. After you went back in to the event."

He looked at her, startled by that revelation. "I didn't know that."

"She's a very special person. I've enjoyed most of our quiet conversations together."

"Most?" he asked, picking up on that one word.

"Yes. There was one night. I believe she was nineteen or twenty years old. She'd just shared her very first kiss with a special man." Inis looked up at him, her eyes sad. "She was devastated."

Rian stiffened in outrage. "I kissed her here, on her twentieth birthday. Are you telling me that she cried because of our kiss?"

Inis shook her head, the sadness weighing heavily on her. "No Rian. She didn't cry because of the kiss. She cried because of what she witnessed after that kiss." She stared up at him. "Do you remember what happened that night? Could she have seen something that might have broken her heart?"

Rian thought back to that night. The guest list had been larger than usual that evening, but there hadn't been any tension during the dinner conversation. He'd seen Amilee sneak out and had followed her. The conversation had been light. Flirty. And the kiss...damn, he still remembered that kiss. He could still taste her, feel her soft, lush curves. Of course, he might also be thinking about last night. Or this morning.

But thinking back to this morning only infuriated him so he pushed the thought away. He didn't want Amilee to leave. He wanted her here. Forever! As his wife, damn it!

"You can't think of *anything* she may have seen?"

Rian blinked, pushing this morning's argument away as he focused back on that long ago night. After the kiss, he'd been called away, needing to review something. He couldn't remember what the issue had been about. He'd intended to resolve the problem, then return to Amilee. He'd even...he'd asked her to wait here. On the bench.

He lifted his head, gazing towards his office.

His office!

Razeen had stopped him in the hallway that night! She'd...hell, she'd pleaded with him to come to her that night. She'd been so desperate, sad, and needy. He'd wanted to push her away but...but she'd begged him. They'd gone into his office...she'd kissed him there. Or tried to!

"Hell!" he muttered, then remembered that his grandmother was still sitting next to him, calmly waiting for him to figure out how he'd messed up so completely. "Sorry."

She patted his hand. "Not a problem, my dear. But I see my work here is done." She stood up and walked down the pathway, back towards the doors. "Go to her and explain what happened that night, correct?" Inis called back over her shoulder as she left the room.

Rian rubbed a hand over his face, then stood and followed her, adjusting his longer stride to her shorter one. "Yes. I..." he couldn't think beyond the stunning realization of what had happened. Amilee had been thinking about that betrayal for years. She'd had plenty of time to let it fester in her heart.

"And you agree that love isn't just a fantasy?" she inquired.

For a long moment, he closed his eyes as everything became clear. "Yes."

She laughed and patted his cheek affectionately. "Good boy. Now go find Amilee and make sure she doesn't get away. I think you two could have a very happy life together."

Rian watched her leave, smiling at the insight she'd shared. She really was a miracle, he thought.

Amilee. Just her name made his body leap to attention. He wanted to see her. No, he *needed* to see her. He needed to explain that night to her. Hell, he needed to explain a lot of things!

He hurried down the hall towards Amilee's room. He'd left her there earlier but he'd been so angry because she'd insisted on leaving, going back to her old life, that he'd left her in a cold fury.

Now that he understood, now that he knew the reason for her resistance to trusting him, he completely sympathized. Hell, he'd be just as upset if she'd gone from kissing him to kissing another man moments later. Damn it, just the thought of her kissing someone else made him hurry faster.

But more than that, he'd hurt her. He'd hurt her so badly that she was still wounded years later. The idea made him sick to his stomach.

By the time he reached her apartment, he was at almost a dead run. He didn't bother to knock. Instead, he burst into the room and looked around for her, terrified she might have left already. He knew that she'd planned to leave in the morning, but it was still a relief to find her sitting by the window. The sad look on her beautiful features tore at him though.

"I'm so sorry!" he blurted out.

Amilee blinked at Rian, wondering why he was breathing so hard. Standing up, she smoothed a hand down over her dress, pushed her glasses higher up onto her nose and tried to pretend as if she wasn't about to burst into tears.

"You're so sorry?" she repeated, pasting on a bright smile. It felt false, but she had to hide her tears. She had nothing left, not even her heart. The only thing left was her pride. "Whatever for? You've been..." she stopped, clasping her hands together as her lips twitched. "I was going to say that you've been a perfect gentleman, but that would be a lie." She chuckled softly. "And I'm very grateful that you weren't."

"Don't!" he blurted, coming to her. Rian took her into his arms and held her close. Amilee closed her eyes, trying to block out the pain but his arms...they were magical. They were strong, amazingly wonderful arms that held her perfectly against his solid, hard body.

"Don't what?" she asked, trying to sound bright and cheerful, but her voice cracked and Amilee had to bury her face against his chest to hide her expression.

"Don't pretend that I'm not a bastard, Amilee. Don't pretend that I didn't hurt you, but damn it, I didn't mean to."

Frantically, she fought back the threatening tears, grateful that he couldn't see her face right now. "I don't think of you as a bastard, Rian. And you haven't hurt me."

He pulled back, his dark gaze locking onto hers. "After that kiss," he said, stopping her attempt to dismiss the pain. "When you were twenty. Our first kiss." He stroked her hair, tilting her head back so that he could smile at her. "I remember every moment of that kiss, Amilee. I've thought about it so many times over the years." He sighed and brushed his lips against her temple. "What I hadn't thought about was Razeen, who cornered me when I was trying to get to my office. And what I hadn't realized was that you'd seen her cornering me."

"That was–"

"That embrace wasn't what you thought it was," he interrupted, not wanting her to dismiss the incident. "Actually, it was exactly what you thought, but only on her side." He kissed her forehead, then stepped back and took her hands. "I didn't want her to touch me, Amilee. I don't know how much you saw, but she was only there briefly. I didn't touch her after she stopped me in the hallway. I didn't go into my office and kiss her. I got away from her as quickly as I could."

"She's a beautiful woman," Amilee stated, looking down at their clasped hands. She should pull away, but she wanted this last connection with him.

"She's not beautiful," he countered. "She's stiff and brittle. She wears so much makeup that I have no idea what she actually looks like. She's mean and self-centered and..."

Amilee's shuddering breath stopped him.

Wet, chocolate eyes looked up at him. Amilee shook her head, her chin trembling as she whispered, "She was your lover at one point. It's obvious that she was. Please don't lie to me."

He sighed, his fingers tightening around hers. "I won't deny it. When we were in college, she and I had a brief affair. A *very* brief affair, which ended almost as soon as it began. I just...I realized that I didn't like her very much."

A tear slipped over her lashes. "You liked her enough to have sex with her. And you liked her enough that you didn't immediately push her away that night."

"That's true, but not because of the reason you think."

Amilee pulled her hands away as she rolled her eyes. "Rian, I highly doubt you know what I'm thinking."

"You think that she followed me back to my office and we had wild sex on my desk."

Amilee froze, unable to stop the stab of pain that lashed at her heart. "I really don't want to hear this, Rian. I should–"

"I love you," he interrupted.

Amilee whipped around, her eyes wide. "Don't!"

He moved closer again, grabbing her hands when she tried to back up. "I love you," he repeated firmly. "And I know you love me. The problem is that I didn't realize I was in love with you. It wasn't Razeen or that night. It's the trust between us, Amilee. You don't trust me because you don't trust my feelings for you."

She nodded. "That's true. I don't trust you."

He smiled. "Fair enough. Amilee, I love you. I didn't realize I loved you until someone very wise pointed it out to me. And," he stopped her when she took a breath to interrupt, "that's not because I didn't believe her. It's because I didn't understand what love was until I met you. No, not just met you, because that happened too long ago. It was that I didn't understand why I wanted you in my life so desperately. Why I am constantly thinking about you. Why I need to hold you, even when we're not going to have sex. Why I love holding you after we make love."

The tears that she'd been holding back welled up and spilled over her lashes. "Don't say things like that, Rian. You don't understand that...."

"That you love me too?" he offered when she didn't continue. He cupped her cheek. "I love you more than I ever thought possible, Amilee. And I'm so sorry that I was such an idiot that I didn't recognize it for so long."

"You didn't love me back then!" she argued hotly.

"Actually, I think I did. I remember that day, the anticipation of seeing you, my eagerness to get you to our bench, to our garden where we always met and had the most wonderful conversations." He kissed her, brushing his lips against hers. But Amilee couldn't respond. She stood stiffly in his arms, afraid that responding would shatter her like glass.

"I didn't understand what love was, Amilee. I didn't know that it was the feeling I had whenever I knew you were about to arrive. I didn't know that it was this aching, yearning to be near you. To touch you. To just see you enter a room. How many times during our visits did we just look at each other across the table and...I knew what you were thinking Amilee. Tell me that you felt it too. That you feel all of it."

"I..."

He kissed her again, feeling her lips tremble slightly with his touch. "If you didn't feel it too, I'll let you go. I'll never contact you again and I'll let you get on with your life." He inhaled and it sounded as if the effort pained him. "But if you feel the same way I do, then please, take a chance on me. On us. Take a chance that we could work out the past hurts and make our future all the stronger."

"I want to but..."

"But Razeen stands in the way."

She closed her eyes. "I keep seeing her touching you, Rian. And every time I see her fingers touching you, I hurt."

He lifted her hands to his chest. "How did she touch me, Amilee?"

She tried to reclaim her hands. But he held them pressed against his chest. "Like this?"

"I don't want to talk about it."

"Please," he urged. "We need to talk about it. I need to erase that memory from your mind. Because I don't remember it. I remember every detail of *our* kiss that night. I remember your laughing eyes when someone said something ridiculous during dinner. I remember the disappointment when you opened the present from me when you were younger, only to find a locket there. And I remember how devastated I felt at seeing that pain in your eyes." Amilee was mesmerized. "So tell me. What did she do? How did she touch me?"

"She reached out and touched your chest, leaning into you."

"Like this?" he asked, brushing her fingers against his chest. "Look at your hand against my chest, Amilee. Look at your fingers. Replace her image with yours. Make a new memory, right here and now."

Amilee looked at her fingers. Softly, she brushed them over his chest, feeling the hard muscles underneath. She felt the heat of him, the power underneath his dress shirt.

"It's you touching me, Amilee. It's you and your hand and your touch that I want. No one else's touch, just yours."

She glanced up at him, then returned her gaze to her hand, moving along the ridges of his chest. She heard him groan, but didn't stop, too mesmerized by the sight of her fingers touching him like this.

"Lean into me, Amilee," he urged, his hands on her hips as he pulled her closer. "Banish every memory except for you and me. I love the way you touch me. Every time I feel your hands on me, I almost explode."

"You do?" she whispered, stunned and more turned on than she'd ever thought possible.

"Yes! I can't believe you don't know that already. I love it when you touch me. And I love it when I touch you. I want to touch every part of you, to know, feel, and explore until I have memorized every inch of your body."

"What if I get fat?"

He laughed, shaking his head. "I adore you, Amilee. You're essential to my daily life. So I don't give a damn what you look like. I will love you as we age, change, and evolve. I will love you when you grow huge with our babies. I will love watching you nurse those babies with your beautiful breasts," and he cupped her breasts, teasing her nipples with his thumbs, making her gasp as the need washed over her.

"You drive me absolutely wild, Rian."

He slipped his fingers underneath her blouse. "You do it to me as well," he told her, taking her hand and pulling it lower. She grasped his erection through his slacks, sliding her hand over him. He shuddered and she felt a surge of power run through her. "Every time you touch me, or even just look at me, I feel like this, Amilee. You have to know that."

"I like making you feel like this," she whispered, her head tilted back so that she could see his face.

"Oh yeah?" he growled. "And what happens when I do this?" he demanded, lifting her blouse over her head, cupping her breasts with his hands, his thumbs caressing the hard tips through her lacey bra. "Or this?" He slid her bra straps down, revealing her breasts so he could latch onto a nipple while his fingers teased the other. "Or this?" he asked, lifting her into his arms. Her legs automatically wrapped around his waist and she felt his erection press against her core as he carried her to the bed.

"Now, I need you naked." He stripped her of every stitch of clothing, then stood back and gazed down at her as he stripped, tossing clothes all over the place in his need to be with Amilee.

"I need you too," she whispered to him, wrapping her arms around his neck and her legs around his waist when he stretched out on top of her.

"I love you, Amilee," he murmured against her lips. He didn't stop kissing her as one hand moved lower, a finger sliding into her wet heat. When he found her slick and ready for him, he had to close his eyes in a valiant effort to control himself.

But it was a wasted effort. Sliding into her, he filled her up, shuddering as her inner muscles tightened around his shaft. "Oh, Amilee, I love you," he groaned, and started thrusting into her, bringing her right to the edge, then pausing to watch the climax overwhelm her. Moments later, his thrusts grew faster as he hurried to follow her. Their breaths mingled, their bodies heating as they climbed higher and higher until...!

"I love you, Rian!" Amilee cried out, tightening her grip around him. That brought him right over the edge and she clung to him as he roared with his release.

Afterwards, he rolled onto his back, bringing her with him as they continued touching each other, enjoying the connection between them.

"You love me," he said, breaking the quiet. A moment later, he laughed, rolling over her so that she was once again under him. "You love me." This was declared with absolute certainty. "I won't take your love for granted, Amilee. Every day, I will prove that I'm worthy of your love."

Amilee reached up and stroked his cheek. "You're more than worthy, Rian. And you don't have to prove anything to me." He twisted his head, kissing her wrist. "I love you."

"Say it again."

"I love you," she replied, then laughed when he nibbled on her neck. "Except when you do that!"

He nipped her earlobe as punishment for that and she laughed even harder. Unfortunately, she couldn't get away because they were still intimately connected, even though she tried.

Suddenly, he stopped and looked down at her, his expression serious. "Amilee, will you marry me? Not because we are betrothed or because of the pressure from our families. Will you marry me because I love you and want to spend the rest of my life making you happy?"

Amilee reached up, sliding her fingers into his dark hair. "Rian, I will marry you. Not because of that ridiculous betrothal contract, or because my father thinks it would benefit the country. But because I love you and want to spend the rest of my life making *you* happy."

His eyes softened as he lowered his head to kiss her. It was the sweetest, most romantic kiss she'd ever experienced. When he lifted his head, he chuckled. "I can't believe how much time we've wasted."

"You're the one who kept letting that woman drape herself all over you." She turned serious. "Don't do it again, Rian. I won't like it and I won't turn away next time."

"There won't be a next time," he vowed. "I promise to keep her well away from the palace and from you. There's no reason for her to be here other than vindictiveness." He kissed her gently. "I have a great deal of power in who actually enters the palace, you know."

She laughed, hugging him. "I know. You're mean that way."

And with that, he threw back his head, laughing.

Epilogue

"Love, why are you sitting out here?" Rian growled, ducking under the branches of the tree as he moved towards Amilee. "That bench can't be comfortable in your condition."

Amilee smiled, rubbing her round belly gently. "I'm just...contemplating," she told him.

Rian sat down next to her, pulling her into his arms so that she leaned against his chest. "Are you feeling okay? I know that you were having pains earlier."

She glanced at him over her shoulder. "How did you...?" she began, then stopped. "My guards have big mouths!" she grumbled.

He laughed, kissing her neck as he covered her hands so they could both rub her belly. "I know. They are overly protective. Go figure."

Amilee shifted, but there wasn't much she could do to find a better position on this hard, marble bench. "They didn't need to tell you."

"You're right," he replied and nipped at her earlobe. "*You* should have told me."

She sighed and shifted again, leaning her head against his shoulder. "But you wouldn't have let me go to the conference."

"Right again. Interesting that you can read my mind so well."

She laughed. "I love you, even when you're being overly protective."

He grumbled. "I love you, even when you're being–"

"Rian!" she gasped, abruptly sitting up as if something had just surprised her.

"What's wrong?" Rian demanded, trying to pull her back into his arms. Immediately, several guards stepped out of the shadows, alert to the possibility of danger.

"Um..." she gasped again, biting her lower lip. "I think that my water just broke. And..." she paused again as pain slashed across her abdomen. "Oh, wow, that's not fun!"

Rian knelt in front of her. "Talk to me, love."

She shook her head, reaching out to grab his shoulder as she leaned forward. For several moments, she couldn't breathe, couldn't speak. All she could do was endure as the pain of her first real contraction pummeled her body. When the contraction eased, she let out a breath, gasping for air and praying that the contractions wouldn't get worse than that one.

She was wrong! Ten hours later, Amilee writhed on the hospital bed, screaming as one contraction after another ripped her apart.

"Okay, Your Highness," the doctor announced, "just one more push! I can see the head. Just one more push and it will be all over!"

Rian gripped Amilee's hand as he bent to look into her eyes. "You can do this, my love. Do it for me."

Amilee screamed, "Not for you! This is for me!" She dredged up the last of her energy and pushed, tears streaming down her cheeks as she begged for relief from this kind of pain. The epidural had worn off about an hour ago and she couldn't wait to meet her baby. And she wanted the pain to stop!

"Perfect!" the doctor called out, making Amilee want to bash his stupid head in. There was nothing "perfect" about this moment!

"It's a boy!" the doctor called out, causing everyone in the room to clap and cheer.

Amilee collapsed back against the pillows, remembering how to breath as relief washed over her. "A boy," she sighed, closing her eyes and pressing her face against Rian's wonderful chest. "A boy."

"Have I mentioned how much I love you?" Rian asked, his voice low and grumbly as he nuzzled her hair with his lips.

"Yeah, well, if you *really* love me, you'll give birth next time," she told him, pressing her cheek against him.

A moment later, a small bundle was placed in her arms and Amilee's tears began in earnest as she gazed down at her precious baby boy. "What will we call him?" she asked, trailing her finger over the infant's cheek, needing to touch him, just to make sure that he was real.

"I don't know. What sounds good with Royal Prince?" he asked, kissing her again and again before kissing the top of his son's head.

"Are Annie and Kate here? They said they'd be here."

Rian kissed her again. "They arrived a couple hours ago. Should I go get them?"

Amilee sighed, shaking her head. "No. Not just yet."

Rian grinned, then added, "Annie brought brownies."

That caught her attention and she looked up, her eyes wide. "Maybe we should see them sooner rather than later!"

Rian laughed, hugging his small family. "That's the woman I love!"

Amilee laughed as well. "You are making fun of me, but wait until you try Annie's brownies!" Then she smiled up at him. "I love you, Rian."

"I love you too, Amilee!"

Message from Elizabeth:

As always, I use my personal observations as inspiration for many stories. The pink dress in this story is no exception. About five years ago, I remember seeing a girl wearing a dress like this in church. She was in the choir and obviously hated being there. She barely sang the song and scowled the whole time.

I'm sure that each of us have a dress, or more specifically, a memory like that one. A memory that is so painful, so embarrassing, that we still remember it decades later. Mine was white stockings – always with a hole in the knees. I was required to wear white stockings to church, but I never had a good pair! Why? Why did I have to wear a torn pair of stockings to church? It was so humiliating!

Anyway – I know that every one of us has a similar story. I love bringing those memories into my stories to share and I hope that the emotions come through to you, the reader.

As always, reviews are vitally important. Would you mind taking just a moment to leave a quick review? You don't have to go crazy on the comments – just a few words would be absolutely wonderful and appreciated! Go back to the book page on your preferred retailer to leave a quick, ten-second review – and thank you!

Again, if you don't want to leave a public review, don't hesitate to email me privately. I answer all emails personally (although sometimes it takes me a few weeks to catch up on all of the messages). Click HERE *to email me directly. (elizabeth@elizabethlennox.com)*

As always, thank you for reading my stories! I truly appreciate each and every one of you!

Elizabeth

(Keep scrolling for an excerpt from Astir's story!)

Excerpt from "The Sheik's Redemption"
Coming April 15, 2022

"Don't you dare!"

Astir del Taran, Sheik of Silar jerked the rifle higher so that it was safely pointing towards the sky as he spun around at the furious command. Since Astir was normally the one giving the commands, hearing the strident voice coming from somewhere behind him was an unwelcome shock. His dark eyes quickly surveyed the area, but he wasn't sure where the angry, feminine voice was coming from. A moment later, he was startled when the bushes rustled, but he still couldn't see the owner of the voice. His guards instantly moved into place, hands resting on the weapons hidden underneath their light coats, out of sight for the moment but easily available if a threat was presented.

A moment later, a beautiful, but angry, female burst through the trees, glaring at him with a stern expression on her surprisingly lovely features. "Do not harm that animal!" she hissed, blue eyes crackling fire.

Astir wasn't sure if he wanted to laugh at the daring woman or...or pull her into his arms and kiss her soft, full lips. His guards promptly ascertained that the female wasn't a threat and faded back into the woods, resuming their vigilance as the woman carefully stepped over branches, weaving around bushes as if she needed to protect every precious leaf and treasured twig.

Astir's eyebrows lifted and he swung his eyes back towards the surprisingly round skunk that was now toddling harmlessly towards his or her den in a hollowed out tree. When he looked at the woman once again, it was to discover that her profile was almost as lovely as her full face. Astir watched her as she watched the skunk escape, oblivious to the danger of his guards or being alone in the woods with a stranger.

"Good. She got away!" the tiny woman sighed, then nodded with relief, as if the world was once again right and happy.

Astir stared at her, not sure what the hell was going on. "You...want...the skunk to live?" he asked, astounded by the mere possibility.

Her crystal blue eyes blinked up at him, causing his mind to blank for a moment.

"Of course I want Jasmine to live!" she replied, her tone implying that she thought his question ridiculous. The woodland beauty waved her hand impatiently towards the log, shaking her head with exasperation. "Why wouldn't I want her to live? She's a beautiful lady!"

What the hell were they talking about? Astir glanced down at her smooth neck, wondering if she'd taste as delicious as she looked. Her bulky sweater didn't do a very good job of hiding the full, round breasts underneath and her leggings hugged soft, enticing thighs. It took every ounce of self-control to stop himself from ordering the woman to turn around so that he could view her derriere. He was certain that the backside of this luscious woman was just as delightful as the front. And yet, she was looking up at him as if he'd lost his mind.

"Why would you want to hurt her?" the strange woman gasped. "Did she try to attack you?"

"She?" he asked, still too absorbed in the beautiful woman's...uh...delights to mentally follow the conversation.

"Jasmine!" the woman replied back, her tone revealing her vexation.

Astir turned his head in the direction of the woman's waving arm. Slowly, his mind began to work. "The skunk?" he asked. "The skunk's name is...Jasmine?"

For the first time, the woman's features showed an emotion other than anger. "Well, yes!"

Astir valiantly suppressed a chuckle. "You named a skunk after...a sweet smelling flower?" Then something else occurred to him. "How do you even know that the skunk is female?"

The lovely, delightful woman shifted on her feet, her arms crossing over her ample chest. "I don't know...exactly...that Jasmine is a female." Her eyes narrowed and that adorable pointed chin lifted in challenge. "But do you know that she isn't a female?"

The beauty had a point, he thought. "Okay, so...*why* are you protecting a skunk?"

Her arms dropped to her side, the fingers clenching into small fists. "Why wouldn't I protect Jasmine? What did she do to you?" the woman snapped, jerking her head towards the area where the skunk had disappeared.

What did she do? Her very existence was an annoyance! "She's a skunk!" he replied, wondering why this was even a question. "She could spray one of my employees!"

The woman snorted, shaking her head with disappointment. But her features cleared and her anger dissipated, morphing into one of patience now. "Skunks are excellent animals to keep around," the woman explained, her tone the same as what she might use if explaining to a toddler. "And if you don't bother them, then they don't spray anyone. Their scent is merely a defense mechanism and they give you several warning signals before they spray."

"Skunks are vermin." Astir settled more comfortably on his feet, enjoying this conversation. He wasn't convinced by her argument, but he liked the sound of her voice. It was soft and feminine, as were those intense, blue eyes and the riot of dark hair that framed her heart-shaped face. His comment had the added benefit of sparking her temper again, creating a flush in those ivory cheeks.

With narrowed eyes and a furious step forward, she shook her head, causing his gaze to move from her gorgeous blue eyes to…well, everywhere! The woman was literally vibrating with fury now.

"Skunks are *not* vermin! They are extremely beneficial to any neighborhood lucky enough to attract one!" she gestured to the area behind him. "They eat real vermin like mice, moles, voles, and bugs! They'll even feast on the termites in a house if they find them, helping homeowners from those destructive creatures. They are omnivores and eat everything that we don't want near our homes!" She shook her head as if disappointed. "I can't believe you would shoot something simply because it might defend itself at some amorphous point in the future! Jasmine wasn't causing anyone harm! She was simply walking back to her home. They are nocturnal, so the only reason you might come across her again is if you're invading her nightly foraging."

The woman stepped closer, her blue eyes changing from angry to pleading. "I'm begging you! Please don't hurt Jasmine. She's just a sweet little lady who only wants to eat mice and bugs and maybe a few leaves and berries. She won't hurt you if you leave her alone."

At this moment, with those eyes staring up at him with such pleading, Astir knew that he'd do anything for this woman. His intense reaction made absolutely no sense, but there it was. He didn't even know her name, and yet, he knew that he'd do just about anything to protect her.

"Your friend will be safe," he promised, surprised by the husky rumble of his voice. His reward for that vow was the most stunning smile he'd ever beheld.

"Thank you!" she whispered, then she stunned him even more by throwing her arms around him and hugging him.

Hesitating a second, Astir shifted the rifle slightly as his free arm wrapped around her back, pulling her in closer as he savored the brief moment of contact.

When she pulled away, Astir wondered what else he could do to feel those magnificent breasts against his chest again. Preferably without the bulky sweater to hinder his enjoyment.

Her face showed a bit of surprise and embarrassment for her enthusiasm of moments ago.

"I'm Rachel, by the way," she explained, then extended her hand, pretending as if she hadn't just wrapped her arms around his waist.

Astir took her hand, enfolding her cold, slender fingers in his own. "Astir," he replied, leaving off his title.

Her eyes sparkled as they shook hands, her lips curling into that delightful smile. "It is a pleasure to meet you, Astir," she said with a bit more formality. For a long moment, they stood there, staring into each other's eyes, their hands clasped. The air seemed to throb with a strange vibration and the early morning sounds disappeared. Then she spoke again and the noises rushed back, his eyes blinking in surprise. "And as a reward for your kindness towards Jasmine, can I offer you a cupcake?" She blushed and Astir was entranced. He'd never seen a woman blush before. The women who had come through his life in the past were too worldly and sophisticated, or perhaps too jaded, to blush.

"A cupcake?" Astir wanted to laugh. For a man who was normally presented with food that could also be considered a work of art, the thought of a simple cupcake was...enticing! Just like every other aspect of this woman standing in front of him.

Rachel couldn't believe what she'd just said. A cupcake? This man was... incredible! Tall and powerfully built, she doubted that the man ever put anything "bad" into his mouth! He probably drank those nasty green protein smoothies for every meal and worked out three or four hours a day. Her body still tingled from that too-brief moment when she'd stupidly hugged him.

"What kind of cupcake?" he asked.

She opened her mouth, but the words seemed to be stuck in her throat. Not to mention, her mind was...not working. Okay, that was a lie. It was working. It simply wasn't working on the right things! Her mind was completely focused on this man's shoulders. And his arms. He had beautiful hands. And a trim waist along with a hard...really hard... chest! That chest, when she'd pressed her face against his chest...yeah a stupid, silly move...she'd felt the scrumptious muscles underneath the expensive wool of his shirt. She'd felt a lot of muscles! What had he asked her again?

"Chocolate?" she offered, but it sounded more like a question.

He stepped closer and his rough, barely handsome features were transformed into an almost boy-like beauty! "Almost" because there was absolutely no way that this big, huge, tall, intensely attractive man could ever be considered a boy. No way! He was just too...male!

"What kind of frosting?" he asked, his deep voice reverential, almost a whisper.

That's when she recognized his expression. The intense desire! For cupcakes? How odd! This big, buff guy wanted cupcakes! Rachel almost laughed with delight.

"You don't look like the kind of man who would eat a cupcake," she commented, feeling a bit more in control now. No, not control. Actually, she wasn't quite sure what she was feeling at the moment. She felt strange and tingly, excited and oddly alive, along with other feelings that she'd never experienced before.

"Chocolate cake is my favorite," he told her, moving even closer. "What kind of frosting?"

"Triple chocolate buttercream," she told him, waiting for…yep! Those dark, mysterious eyes lit up with eagerness!

He was in love! Oh, not in love with her. Rachel didn't fool herself into believing that a man like this could fall in love. He was too tough, too manly and harsh, and yet…!

But he was definitely in love with the concept of a double chocolate cupcake. With a grin that she didn't know was delightfully mischievous, she leaned forward slightly and whispered, "I also filled the center with chocolate cream."

She watched, fascinated as his jaw clenched and his eyes burned brighter. Was he really that tempted?

"Woman, give me a cupcake or…" he looked over at the log where Jasmine was most likely sound asleep. "Or I'll wake up your friend and…"

"Don't you threaten Jasmine," Rachel interrupted, then laughed because she could see that he wouldn't harm the adorable skunk. Jasmine was safe enough, from this man at least. "Come on. The cupcakes are all yours."

"Lead the way," he said, gesturing with his free hand, the rifle still leaning against his shoulder, safely pointed towards the sky.

Printed in Great Britain
by Amazon